No One Left

By: Mary Reason Theriot

Dedication

Without the love and support of my family and friends, I would not have pursued this new path in life. I would especially like to thank those that have proofread copy after copy, to give me their honest opinion of the books.

To my daughter Theresa, thank you so much for your continued encouragement.

To my wonderful husband Malwen, your continued love and support mean the world to me. I don't know what I would do without you in my life. All of my books wouldn't be what they are without you pushing me forward.

To my fans, I would like to offer a special thank you for your continued support.

Professionally edited by Little House of Edits and proofed by Proofreading by the Page.

ISBN-10: 1-945393-02-5
ISBN-13: 978-1-945393-02-0

Also Available by Mary Reason Theriot:

The Hideaway

The Traveler

Dr. Frankenstein

Above Suspicion

Horror in the Night

Deadly Seduction

Echoes on the Bayou

Seven Deadly Sins

A Kiss So Deadly

A Deadly Combination

CarnEvil of Souls

Seduced by Voodoo

www.maryreasontheriot.com

Prologue

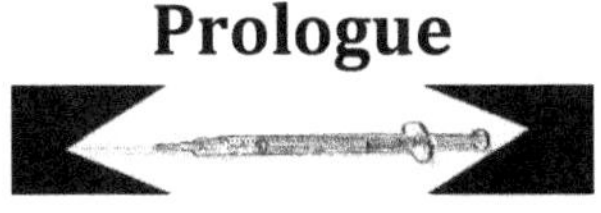

Dead. Until now, his life had no meaning but that one little word would mark the importance of it.

As in his life, he was all alone in death. No one would miss him. No one was here to watch him die; to watch him take his final gasp of air. No one was here to notice just how sick he was.

There were no kind hands to hold his. There was no one here to show others he was loved. There was no one to reach out and close his eyelids or to cover his cold blue face.

All of his life, he wanted someone to care for him and love him for who he was. But now, with his death, he would finally have someone pay attention to him. They may not know his name, but they would know one thing, he was the first to die. With his single death, he would start a chain reaction.

Chapter 1

An elite group of four men, including the President of the United States, Michael Edwards, had met six months ago at a hotel conference room in late December. Now that it was after reelection, it was time for them to meet again. He had wanted a second term so that he could pursue his current agenda and, thanks to the American public, he was given just that opportunity.

Tonight, they were meeting in a hotel room here in D.C.. None of them could ever be seen at the same time in the White House. They sat comfortably in the living room of the luxurious suite and talked about their most current project.

President Edwards has spent a considerable amount of time working on ways to lower the deficit, but to date, this was the best plan they have come up with. "As we all know, the deficit is growing expeditiously. We have to do something about it now or we will be in debt to other countries for generations to come. This is the only answer," President Edwards explained.

Kevin Jameson passed out the research reports while explaining, "These are the numbers from our research groups. If you notice, the government is spending more and more each month on Social Security payments, including those receiving disability. With the economy's present condition, unemployment is also up. Americans are living longer these days; it will not take long for the funds in Social Security to completely run out."

President Edwards looked around the room and announced, "Men and women are no longer retiring at the age of 65. Instead, they are collecting their social security, retirement, and holding down part time jobs. This plan will not only reduce the deficit, but it will also open up more jobs; hence, decreasing the number of people drawing unemployment."

General Gregory Thompson, M.D., a military man who even at fifty-five kept himself in top form, looked at the report. He managed to move up in the Army ranks because he was good at taking orders without question. Being raised in a military household, it was essential for Gregory to live by the rules his dad demanded. If not, the punishment would be severe. Thompson had always been intrigued with germ warfare and all the nasty little bugs associated with it, which was one of the reasons he made sure that his grades were well above average. He never missed a day from school nor did he allow himself to get anything other than an A+. From an early age, he decided that he would enlist in the Army, hoping to develop vaccines which would eventually be used in germ warfare by the U.S. Armed Services. By the time he enlisted, he knew everything there was to know about anthrax and other deadly contagions. He made sure to impress all the right people, but just as importantly, he always followed orders when given to him.

He was good at his job. As second in command, he was one of the top leaders. Nothing stood in his way to achieve his orders. He was ruthless; which was one of the reasons he was chosen for this particular mission.

As a matter of fact, he spent most of his career as not only a military medical doctor, but an expert in molecular biology.

He served at the U.S. Army Medical Research Institute of Infectious Diseases, USAMRIID for short, at Fort Detrick, Maryland. The work he was allowed to do there had been right up his alley, with the vaccines being the perfect biological weapon. The Chief of Staff had highly recommended him for this particular group, which was an honor for him.

With an accusatory glare, Thompson stated, "We must pick the group carefully. We can afford no leaks of any sort."

Kevin Jameson nodded his head, knowing that if anything went wrong, his head would be the one to roll. President Edwards would make sure that he did not go down for what they were planning.

For the past ten years, Kevin ran the clandestine errands for this particular group. He has done countless unpleasant things that went with the job. He has been privy to a fair share of secrets; secrets that could be used to bribe one with or even cause one to be killed over.

The people in this group did not care how Kevin did what he did; they only wanted results. That was something he was exceedingly good at; except, this time he found this particular order hard to swallow.

These men believed they knew him so well; they thought they knew his weaknesses. He only allowed them to know what he believed was necessary. Underneath his bland façade was a cunning mind perfectly suited to the duplicitous, infinitely complicated world of espionage.

Defensively, Kevin stated, "We will be using the Unacknowledged Special Access Project department, USAP. Randy Erickson is as ruthless as we are and I trust the men and women he assigned to this project."

President Edwards rose and began to pace the room, "If the American public ever finds out what we are doing, it will be the death of us all. We have seen the numbers and there is no other way out of this deficit without selling our soul to a third world country. I refuse to do that since we have a simple solution here in our possession."

Kevin felt his stomach begin to knot as he listened to the President's speech. He was trained not to feel fear, but he was feeling a sensation right now that surprised and annoyed him. He never had a problem sentencing a guilty man to death, but an innocent man being sentenced to death? That was hard for him.

With a hesitant, uncertain voice, Daniel Wright asked, "Are we sure this is the only way to handle this problem?"

Without even bothering to turn and face the man, President Edwards stated in a clear, angry voice, "This is the only way to end this problem as far as I am concerned. In the last six months, no one else has been able to give me a plan that will decrease the deficit like this one."

Straightening his tie, President Edwards informed the men, "Now, if you don't mind, I need to get ready for a press conference at four o'clock. I do not want to keep the public waiting."

As the President's disdainful demeanor filled the room, the men glanced at each other before stating in unison, "Yes, sir."

As he strode out of the room, the men looked at the closed door. After a few moments, Daniel looked over at the other men; he was unsure of how to handle any of this. He adjusted his tie and mopped at the perspiration building on his brow. With deliberate slowness, he unhooked his steel rimmed bifocals one ear at a time and laid them on the highly polished coffee table in front of him. All he kept thinking was, "what if they get caught?" He didn't remember signing up to commit this type of atrocity. As his thoughts bewildered him, he began to feel disheartened, as the terrible truth of the situation became real. "I am not so sure now that his re-election was a good thing. That is all I have thought about lately."

An uncomfortable silence built up in the room. Thompson looked at Daniel and then the other men before stating, "If any of you want out, now is the time to say something."

Thompson knew that Daniel may be a problem. If any of them were to grow a conscience, it just may be Daniel. "We all know that Edwards hasn't taken this plan lightly. He thought about it for quite a long time before deciding to present this proposed plan to us. We should all be honored just to be considered trustworthy enough to attend this high level discussion."

As Kevin listened to Thompson ramble on, he had to hold back laughing in disgust and rolling his eyes. The man was truly a brown noser, but one that only did so for his own personal gain. If there wasn't anything in it for Gregory, he wouldn't even consider being a part of this particular team.

Kevin quickly reminded all of the men there, "None of this can be done until the research is finalized and Edwards gives the final authorization."

Daniel listened to the men talking, but found his mind drifting. How the hell did he end up in this mess? When he heard the original proposal months ago, he thought it would never even be considered a second time. Even now, none of them truly knew exactly what was planned. Edwards has been spewing more half sentences, trying to avoid telling any of them exactly what he has planned. Daniel wondered just how many half lies Edwards has told, not only to the American public, but this group as well. It was as if he truly didn't want them to know just what he has planned.

Daniel had a feeling that if he were to ask each man what Edwards had ordered each of them to do, each would have a different task. He felt the President would not fully advise any of them of his true plans until the last minute.

Clearing his throat, Daniel reminded the men, "We all know that what is being proposed is illegal."

Waving his hand, Thompson stated, "Spare me the sob stories. Very few of the things we actually do are legal; besides, orders are orders."

Daniel didn't feel right doing something that was definitely illegal and went completely against the Constitution of the United States. He could hear the whining in his voice even as his temper rose. What they planned to do was clearly un-American. "This proposal will possibly end millions of lives. Are we certain that what he is proposing would be contained within this small group and not spread to others?"

Kevin stood up and explained, "The scientists are working on that at this very minute. We are using a self-contained facility to make sure that it does not spread."

Daniel still wasn't convinced. "And just how do they do that?"

Kevin informed them, "Basically, the scientists are developing a way for the virus to die once it has moved through the host's blood system."

Thompson looked at the men. "Besides, who in the hell will think twice about a bunch of elderly and sick developing a bad case of the flu? Every year someone dies from a simple case of the flu. This is the perfect set up; the perfect way to end their sucking the economy dry. I admit that it may seem inhumane, but it is the best way to help us remove the problem with the deficit. Just remind yourselves that these people have lived their lives to the fullest already."

As Daniel listened to Thompson explain the problem, he suspected that even they may be included along with the sick and elderly as expendable.

***

Gregory Thompson let himself into his private suite before picking up his disposable cell phone. The late afternoon sun streamed through the open windows. As he waited for the other line to answer, he closed the drapes.

Their current President was a natural politician, but he wasn't a very smart man. So far, the greatest skill he has shown was appointing very smart, yet ruthless, men to support him. He thought he was in control, but little did the President know, he was being manipulated by some very powerful, dangerous men from the shadows.

Finally, the voice on the other end drawled out, "Yes."

"The President is going forward with the plan, just as you presumed."

A deep chuckle reverberated over the line, "Good. Do you foresee any problems?"

"There is one that I do believe is developing a conscience."

"Hmm, I suggest you watch him closely. If need be, eliminate any problems before they become too big to handle."

"Yes, sir."

Chapter 2

The days and nights all rolled into one. Faces became a blur, a miasma of a memory. None of this made any sense. He was no longer sure how long he has been used as a pin cushion. He wasn't sure if this was even happening; it could just be one long nightmare.

He heard the footsteps echo down the halls. The only thing he did know for certain was they would come for him once more. When he tried to lift his head, the room began to spin. Nausea overcame his body. Would this be the day he died?

He was afraid to close his eyes. With each passing day, the nightmares became more intense, frightening. He could feel things crawling up his body. He thrashed his legs, hoping that the bugs would scurry away, but the sheets stuck to his sweat soaked body.

His jail cell opened. He blinked as a face appeared in front of him. Rough hands slid under his arms, dragging him onto a cold gurney.

He could feel the straps restrain him and heard the click of the handcuffs. He watched the overhead lights speed by, as they made their way down the hallway.

The cheap cotton sheet tangled around his legs and dropped off the gurney onto the cement floor. He moaned and started to fall into unconsciousness when he felt the needle being jabbed into his arm.

The darkness he was forced to suffer through had varying degrees to it. There were times when everything around him was so dark that he could not detect even a shadow of movement, but free from pain. Then there was another version where his world was a mixture of black and gray, but he could feel some of the pain his body was experiencing.

He carefully opened his eyes, as the fog he has been under lifted. In front of him was a mutated form, half black with streaks of gray. He closed his eyes again; the pain in his body dwindled as well as the aching. He could feel every beat of his heart, and it felt as if his insides were on fire.

Opening his eyes once more, the shapes in front of him began to come into focus. The coldness of the room slowly helped him piece together where he was located. He was back in the room he dreaded. He tried to move his body, only to be reminded that he was secured to the gurney.

"Please... please, I beg of you, no more." The words came out as nothing more than a tortured whimper. His voice no longer sounded human, but that of a tortured animal.

The doctor looked over at the woman standing in the doorway. "His white cell count is dropping. I think we may have the correct ratio."

Suddenly, he began to convulse as a cold sweat formed on his body. He could feel the fever quickly rising. Death was finally near.

He tried to scream out in pain as he fell into a dark abyss, but his lips only dribbled sputum. A cocoon of coldness enveloped him as death closed in.

The doctor murmured quiet observations, as the orderly moved on. Dr. Trey Welsh looked down at the patient covered in sweat stained sheets. His limbs now had a mind of their own, desperately trying to find coolness, as the oppressive fever consumed his body. The scent of death hung heavy in this area of the prison.

With gloved hands, he secured a tourniquet to the upper arm of one of the other patients. He extracted two vials and a syringe from his coat pocket. Skillfully, he inserted the needle into the patient's vein, while adjusting it slightly until he saw the flow of blood. Once the second tube was filled, he capped it and placed it into the small insulated bag he has concealed on him.

Speaking quietly through his mask, he told the moaning patient, "This will all be over soon."

No sooner than he said the words, the patient began gasping for his last breaths on this earth. Once the last patient passed away, he sat down at his makeshift desk to jot down his notes. "Initial dosage failed. All six subjects survived. Second dosage was more successful. Two subjects expired a week later. Third dosage was successful. All subjects deceased. No other prisoners have shown signs or symptoms of the virus."

Closing his notebook, he shoved away from his desk. The remaining money he was owed would be deposited into his account today. By tomorrow, he would be off to a faraway island and starting a new life. All thanks to the United States Government.

***

At well past midnight, the disposable cell phone shrilly rang in the pristine office. "Yes?"

The man stated, "Everything is in place, sir. All we need is your go ahead."

President Edwards closed his eyes and blocked out what he was about to do. This was for the good of the country. Once the order was given, there would be no turning back. "Yes."

The man confirmed, "It shall be done then, sir."

As the caller hung up, Edwards whispered into the darkness, "God help us all."

Chapter 3

Miranda Hamilton smiled as she eyed herself in the full length mirror once more. She still looked good for her age. Her skin was a flawless work of art, thanks to the makeup that was painstakingly applied. Even in the bright daylight, her skin was as smooth as a soft petal from a flower.

She used a little mascara to darken her naturally long lashes. A hint of blush to her high cheekbones enhanced her color. She pulled her long, shoulder length hair up into a tight bun to keep it out of her way while working. She had considered cutting it short, but with long hair, she could change the style whenever she felt like it. If she were to cut it short, she would then be forced to wear her hair in only one simple style.

She added a pair of gold hoop earrings to the ensemble. The earrings gave the outfit just the right amount of sparkle without interfering with her work. Today, she was dressed in a midnight blue skirt and a soft white silk blouse. She slipped on a pair of black heels and headed to work.

She has worked in the Unacknowledged Special Access Project department, USAP, for going on ten years now. The United States Government used them to control sensitive research programs.

Miranda has often wondered about her choice of careers lately. Working for USAP could be compared to a jail sentence. She was allowed limited contact with her peers. And even her incoming and outgoing information was closely monitored and regulated. Miranda also suspected that she was being followed. Security was not only intimidating, but brutal at times. There were cameras that followed your every step outside and inside the building. Even in the bathrooms you had no privacy. She has learned this was not the place to ask questions, just do as you were told.

Later that day, her supervisor called her in for a last minute meeting. As she sat across the table from the others, she cringed as they cracked jokes and laughed. It was hard for her to wrap her mind around how they could even think about joking with what their current project was.

When her supervisor, Randy Erickson, walked into the room, she could barely muster a smile. Her heart pounded as he sat down. Everyone in the room went quiet, as they waited for him to speak.

She was being held back in this profession, but not because she lacked intelligence, didn't have enough degrees behind her or that she lacked dedication. What held her behind was that she still had a soul or at least somewhat of a conscience.

Randy Erickson looked directly at her, "Now Miranda, you are certain that this flu will not be a contagion?"

She nodded her head before replying, "From all the research that I have reviewed, there is no way that this flu will become viral. Once it is introduced into the patient, it attacks the body quickly, but it dies before it can spread."

A frown formed across Randy's face, as he thought of what she said, "And you are certain that there is no risk of contagion?"

Jasper Conway cleared his throat and answered, "Sir, two inmates were infected and none of the other prisoners developed the virus. The hosts died before they had a chance to pass it on."

Miranda looked over at Jasper. As he smiled at her smugly, what she wouldn't do to wipe that look off of his face. He never even bothered to tell her that they were doing further tests on the vaccine, much less the virus being added to it.

Randy looked over at Miranda. "You will be in charge of the vaccine distribution schedule. We have to guarantee that only the designated sites get it. We do not want to be accused of killing innocent people after all."

Miranda couldn't help but smirk at that comment. Oh no, they wouldn't want to kill off the ones they considered worthy of living, just the elderly and sick. It was almost as if they were playing God; actually to be more exact, they were the Devil's Advocate.

This whole project was still too unbelievable. This was America and the government was not supposed to sacrifice people; yet, here they were discussing that very thing. If word of this would ever get out, the scandal would ruin all of them.

As the meeting continued, Miranda mused about the illness they would be injecting into unsuspecting people. What would happen if the public were to ever find out what was unleashed on the people by the government and where the exact order came from? Has anyone even thought about the implications of what they were doing?

The worse thing that could possibly happen was if the trials were wrong and this contagion spread to others. Miranda's attention was drawn to the table, as Randy spread out a large printout. "These are the numbers that you all have been working on. It will be required protocol before anyone receives the free vaccine. They must show not only their identification card, but their Social Security or Medicare card as well. Only after the recipient's identification is confirmed, will the vaccine be administered."

Conway looked over the group before adding, "Several operatives have been handpicked to insure that distribution protocols are met."

Randy continued on. "Do we have documented results that show there have been no survivors from the vaccine as of yet?"

Miranda took a deep, modulated breath and hoped that no one noticed her unease, "No, not as of yet. We have various scientists and researchers working on this particular project without any of them truly knowing what they are actually working on. So far, all the results have been the same; the vaccine will kill whoever it is given to."

Conway interrupted again, "This particular virus moves quickly through the blood system. It attacks the brain and damages it beyond repair from lack of oxygen shortly after the virus is injected."

Miranda reminded those attending the meeting. "There will be no reversing the effects of the vaccine once injected. The patient's mind will never be revived and the cells of the body will be too damaged to restore."

Randy asked, "Are we certain that the scientists and researchers working on this particular project have no idea what is going on?"

 "Yes," Conway answered, "They have been informed that they are working on a potential virus that is just in the theoretical stage at this time. No one outside of our circle knows that the virus will actually be administered through the vaccine."

Randy looked around the room, "If any of you do not have the stomach for what we are about to do, I suggest you go lock yourself in your office now."

Conway nodded his head. "I admit that this is some crazy shit, but all of us here have been with the agency for a while now and we all know how to handle the sensitive cases."

Miranda wanted to roll her eyes. They believed that what they were about to do was for the good of the country, but no matter how they tried to justify their actions, she didn't see how this was in the best interest of the country. But any objections on her part at this time would merely sign her death certificate. She was just as guilty as the rest of them simply by being a part of this and knowing about the plans. For now, it was best to play along with everything.

Randy stated, "I know that all of you have always gone above and beyond what we have expected of you, but this time, we are going to be doing something that most individuals will consider inhumane. If any of you have any doubts, that is fine, but I do need you to swear that you will stick your head in the sand and keep your eyes and mouth shut."

Even as Randy looked at everyone nodding their head in agreement, he had his doubts. He said a silent prayer that they have not all just signed their death certificates. With something as volatile as what they were doing, they more than likely have already signed their lives away. The government would not want any witnesses, period.

***

After a restless night, Miranda stumbled into work. As she approached her office, she pressed her face against an optical sensor that scanned her retinas. Once approval had been recognized by the computer, her office door was opened. Her current assignment was so top secret that limited access was made available to office personnel. Even her secretary was not allowed in her office for the time being or even allowed access to her computers. Heidi was better off that way. If she were to know what was being planned, Miranda had no doubt it would wear a hole in her stomach just as it was doing with her.

The man sitting at her desk was handsome, yet she wondered why he was here. She was surprised to find someone already in her office.

Kevin Jameson stood up to welcome her; it was imperative that he speak with her. He was counting on his suave mannerisms to help put her at ease as he explained the next phase of the project.

As with all his meetings, he wore his usual dark suit. This allowed him to pass as an intelligence officer without ever being questioned. Anonymity was imperative in this business.

In his line of work, stress could be overwhelming at times, but until this latest project, he had no desire to change jobs. His employer made sure to treat its most valued employees like royalty. They offered extremely lucrative salaries and exceptional benefits package. This was the first time he has ever questioned if the money was worth it.

Miranda Hamilton was not what he had expected. She was statuesque and even with her hair in a tight bun. There was no hiding that she was a very attractive woman. This was the kind of woman who would help ease work stress. He could spend hours worshipping her body; unfortunately, he never mixed business with pleasure.

As she brushed past him, he could feel her body heat. The smell of her perfume was intoxicating. He had done his research on this Miranda Hamilton; he knew she had no boyfriend or husband, which was such a shame.

He moved out of her way and informed her, "The President of the United States is pleased with the results. The project has been approved. You are to proceed with the utmost caution. There is to be no computer documentation with regards to this project; there will only be a paper trail."

A shiver of fear ran through Miranda as she heard his words. She had heard the reasoning behind this particular project, but she never thought it would come to fruition. These victims were not seen as people; instead they were considered to be only weak, financial drains on the economy. Their reasoning behind this method was it would save the government millions, maybe billions, in social security and welfare distributions.

Kevin Jameson handed Miranda a packet. "In here is your new identity. Your cover will be as a top executive of the Department of Health and Social Services. We made arrangements for you to have a mobile medical unit that disburses the inoculations. Given the importance of discretion, you will be the one who travels to each of the health centers for distribution." Kevin looked her and asked, "Now, what I need to know is if you will be able to infect those as planned?"

Miranda swallowed back her fears, "I will leave when you tell me."

"You are to leave in the morning." With that comment, he turned on his heel and walked out the door.

Miranda wondered if he had the same doubts as her. Did he question the logic of this decision as well?

***

"Sir, the feeds are up and running. If you will follow me."

The control center of this operation was buried deep underneath the oval office. It was nothing more than a cramped space, filled with screens showing each of the monitored team members. None of them even knew that they were injected with a tracking device and they would never know.

Each monitor has a code name scrawled beneath their respective monitor. It had been so easy to inject the GPS tracking device on each of the members. The small device was added to the vaccines they received at the beginning of the project. It was easy to convince them the importance of receiving the vaccination. After all, they were going to be around some deadly viruses.

The man manning the room's sophisticated electronics leapt to his feet as his supervisor and guest entered. With a dismissive wave, he slipped out of the office briefly.

"We will be able to track their every movement."

Chapter 4

The last rays of the sun were now gone and thousands of stars shimmered weakly against a dark sky. Few street lights illuminated the night. The roads were littered with trash. This region of Portland, Oregon housed the poorest of the population and was well below the nation's standards.

Headlights suddenly appeared in the darkness and briefly illuminated the sparse shrubbery that lined the yards. The battered Ford truck ground its gears as it bounced on the heavily potholed road. Drawn by the flickering beams of light, insects swarmed towards the truck splattering against the dust streaked windshield.

Hillcrest Pines Housing lay just on the outskirts of Portland, Oregon. The residents here were a diverse group, but the one thing they all had in common was they were low income families; some were several generations' poor.

Kim Langley knew for certain that the residents here did not care about their housing situation. Graffiti decorated most of the homes' exteriors. Several cars sat on cement blocks; the grass around them had not been cut in a very long time. Screens from the windows hung askew and duct tape barely held the window glass in place.

The housing complex consisted of three rows of homes forming a wide "U" around a worn courtyard, which has seen better days.

Kim adjusted the oversized black nursing bag on her shoulder as she walked towards one of the houses. If it had not been for her watching her own mother suffer from cancer, she wondered if she would have chosen a different career.

As she neared the front door, she realized she forgot to apply the menthol rub under her nose that helped to block out the odors in places such as this. The overpowering smell of unwashed bodies, cigarette smoke, and alcohol filled the air here.

Her newest patient, Mr. Roy Bowman, was bedridden and his family had difficulty caring for him. As with all of her patients, they came from recommendations from a concerned relative.

She knocked on the door and waited for one of Mr. Bowman's children to answer. They had assured her that someone would be here to greet her.

Kim was surprised to see a woman in her sixties open the door. The woman's hands were almost claw like from arthritis and her body was cringed over from the ravages of time. She looked at Kim with concern in her eyes. "You must be the home health nurse my brother, Junior, asked to come. He asked me to come let you in. I told Junior that I could take care of our dad, but he insisted we use the insurance to its fullest."

She opened the door to allow Kim to enter. It was stifling inside the tiny house and there was a distinct odor of cat urine that attacked the senses. "Sorry about the heat. Dad was complaining that he was cold and wanted the blasted heat turned up high."

Moving through the house, the old woman called out, "Well, let me show you Dad's room." Calling out over her shoulder she explained, "It's this way."

Kim noticed the way the woman limped, favoring her left side. Kim suspected that she had a stroke sometime in the past and never sought medical attention. From the looks of the house, it appeared that Mr. Bowman's family barely took care of him.

As they made their way to the bedroom, Kim informed her, "Since your father is a new patient, I will need to do an initial assessment."

"I understand that," replied the daughter.

Kim peeked into the room and was taken aback by what she saw. Her newest patient appeared to be a very sick man. "How long has he been like this?"

The daughter shook her head, "He wasn't like this last night when I went to bed. Junior took him to get a flu shot just yesterday." The daughter began to stammer as she explained, "I didn't come back until right before you got here."

Picking up her father's hands, she asked, "Daddy, are you okay?" The daughter looked back at Kim, "He's burning up with fever."

***

By the end of the day, Kim was ready to go home, crawl into her bed, and eat a pint of chocolate ice cream. She looked at her patient list, though, and saw that she had one more patient to see. She prayed that this patient wasn't as sick as the others she had cared for today. Three of the six she has seen so far had to be admitted to the hospital and that meant tomorrow she wouldn't have her usual load or pay.

Before heading to the next house, she stopped at a local coffee shop drive thru and ordered a white chocolate mocha. She needed a caffeine fix before going to her next appointment. She paid one of the strangest cashiers she has ever seen. The man's head was shaved and his entire body seemed to be covered with intricate tattoos. He had more rings and studs protruding from his earlobes, nose, and lips than she owned. She wondered how he even managed to get this job, but then again you could not judge a book by its cover.

As she took a sip of the hot coffee, she let the warmth of the drink spread through her body. Even with the heater on in her small car, she could feel the biting cold of winter in her bones.

Her last patient was Mrs. Delores Franklin, her favorite patient. She knocked on the door before entering the house. "Mrs. Franklin, it is Kim."

Kim was surprised to find Mrs. Franklin still in bed. Fear coursed through her, as she looked at the woman's glassy stare. It appeared that another of her patients had come down with the flu. Taking the elderly woman's hand in hers, she asked, "How are you doing, Mrs. Franklin?"

Mrs. Franklin forced out her words, "I don't feel so good. My daughter brought me into town yesterday for my shot and shopping. I guess it was too much for me."

As a coughing fit overcame her, Kim helped her sit up in bed, "Mrs. Franklin, I need to take your temperature. I believe you have a high fever."

Before heading home, Kim made two calls. The first one was for an ambulance to bring Mrs. Franklin to the hospital and the other call was to her daughter. After letting the daughter know that her mom was being transported to the hospital, Kim headed home with a heavy heart. She has never treated so many people sick with the flu in one day in all of her career. It was like nothing she has ever seen before.

At least she received her flu shot early this year. It appeared that this would indeed be a bad flu season. Could it be that the government also feared this and that was the reason they were offering so many of the vaccines for free? Perhaps they hoped that it would keep the epidemic from spreading too much.

Chapter 5

This was literally the biggest job she has been given and Miranda could do little to control her nerves. She forced on a smile and tried to look confident. She was getting ready to commit a capital crime at the request of the U.S. government.

She tried to radiate authority as she made her way to the travel trailer. She took painstaking care this morning to make herself look like a doctor in control. As she made her way to the tiny office, she noticed that the line was already long.

Two of the elderly patients murmured hello to her and she smiled back to them. Those in line glanced at her. She let out a sigh of relief when no one questioned why she was here. She looked like she belonged here. Before she began sentencing these very people she just smiled at to death, she forced herself to calm down.

Her heart pounded against her chest as she swiped her ID at the door. Inside the tiny travel trailer that was set up as a mobile medical unit, she found herself facing a line of bared forearms and wondered just how many of these people she would manage to kill today. Her thoughts were quickly interrupted by the next patient in line.

An elderly man raised his shirt sleeve and waited for his shot. These twelve hour days were starting to weigh heavy on Miranda. She has lost count of how many people she inoculated today alone. She no longer even knew what day it was.

She looked at the calendar and shuddered when she saw it was only Tuesday. This was only her second day inoculating everyone with the vaccine.

Once she gave the elderly man his shot, she made a notation in her booklet of his name, date, and time. For this particular part of the mission, there would be no computer data, paper documentation only.

More forearms appeared in front of her. This time it was a young mother with an infant. Her assistant handed her another vial. Miranda prepared the next inoculation and begged God to forgive her for what she was doing.

This girl was so thin that as she pushed the syringe into her arm, she actually hit bone. Miranda informed the young girl, "You may feel sick for a little bit this afternoon, but it should pass by the morning."

"Thank you, ma'am. What about the baby?"

Miranda shook her head and replied, "He is too young."

As another set of forearms appeared before her, she gave yet another. This time, though, there was no thank you and the man just rushed out the door.

As she continued, she wondered if God would protect them from what she has done.

That night as Miranda drifted off to sleep, the faces danced through her mind. She made a decision; she would save the last vial for herself and prayed that God had mercy on her soul.

***

The disposable cell phone rang. As he looked at those seated in his pristine office, he said, "I need to take this."

Without questioning their boss, they filed out of the room. Once the room was cleared, he answered the phone, "Yes?"

"It has started."

President Edwards asked, "All went according to plan?"

"Yes, sir. The deaths have already started. It won't be long before everyone given the vaccine will no longer be a problem."

Chapter 6

Sadie Wilson was tired. It has been a long, rotten night. She hated working the night shift and tonight was no different. She has exactly five minutes left until the end of her shift, but before she headed home, she had to check on Mrs. Delores Franklin for her friend, Kim Langley. She was ready to get the hell out of here. She already had a run in with one of the obnoxious doctors working tonight and would rather not run into another. It wasn't her fault that the doctor could not read simple English. There was no reason for him to verbally light into her the way he did. She has been writing chart notes longer than this doctor has been practicing.

She was a damn good nurse, but being confronted by a doctor always had her doubting her skills. When she was being belittled, her brain seemed to shut down. All she could do was stand there unable to defend herself.

As she replayed the conversation in her mind once more, her stomach grew tight. She walked into the elderly woman's room and instantly knew that it wasn't good. Without even thinking, she went into action. Acting on instinct alone, she called the code and prayed that they could save this woman.

****

Dr. Brandon Collins let out a long sigh as he left the deceased's room. He has never seen anything like this. He has admitted plenty of patients for a simple flu, but this particular strain seemed to kill the patients faster than they could diagnose them.

Just today alone, he admitted eleven patients and three of those have already passed away in the last eight hours.

As Dr. Russell Morris relieved him from the night shift, he informed him, "It appears to be a pretty serious strain of influenza. So far, eleven people have been admitted and three of those are deceased."

"Is it contained? Do we need to contact the Center for Disease Control?"

"I have been too busy to check with other hospitals, much less contact the CDC. Whatever this is, it is progressing fast, too fast."

Dr. Morris asked, "Do you think we should be concerned that the virus is hot?"

Sighing, he replied, "I pray it isn't."

A hot virus was an airborne virus that all medical professionals feared. It was nearly impossible to contain and a true nightmare. The only safe course of action was to quarantine the patients.

Chapter 7

Kevin Jameson met Gregory Thompson at the Dixie Grill to discuss the previous group meeting. They found a table in the back where they could discuss the events in relative quiet, away from prying ears. The background noise of the various televisions being used to entertain the variety of clients helped to drown out their conversation.

The television near the two men was playing the evening news. On the screen was a young female news reporter talking about the local hospital having seen the first flu patients of the season.

Kevin looked over at Thompson, "You were a little rough on Daniel the other day."

"Not as rough as I should have been. You should have been a little more forceful as well. He can turn out to be a real problem, you know." With a hard edge to his face, he added, "I also think he is hiding something. He keeps evading all of my phone calls."

That very thought worried Kevin more than he would ever let on. He also felt that Daniel was hiding something. He hoped that the man hasn't decided to try to redeem his bad acts by informing the public of what they were doing.

As the waitress refilled their drinks, the two men paused their conversation. They were all fully aware of the secret nature of any of their meetings and they must make sure to behave accordingly. In their silence, they heard the newsman's broadcast. "With an update to Sandra's story that ran earlier, there is confirmation of the first death associated with this season's flu." The man's pleasant, well-modulated voice was clearly audible over the clinking of glasses and muted conversations. "We would like to remind everyone that the flu vaccine is available. This is the best prevention method. The vaccinations are one hundred percent safe with minimal side effects." From the corner of the view, a nurse holding a hypodermic needle moved next to the news reporter. She began to remove a pink liquid from a vial into the syringe. Taking an alcohol pad, she rubbed his forearm briskly before plunging the needle into his skin. "To show you just how safe I believe the vaccination is, I have asked Nurse Connelly with Mercy General to give my inoculation on air." He smiled over at the nurse and thanked her for her service before looking at the camera once more. "Now, Wendy has tonight's forecast for you."

Thompson turned to Kevin and asked, "You believe that Daniel is hiding something too, don't you?"

Kevin's expression turned harsh as he replied, "I'm convinced he should be watched closely. It is hard to see this man as being diabolically clever. I think he just acts and looks nervous, but something about his demeanor doesn't sit well with me. He could be double talking and if that is the case, I don't like that."

Reaching for his drink, Thompson nodded his head. "There is a reason each of us was picked for this group; we are all ruthless at our job."

Kevin informed him, "I asked Daniel Wright to meet us here tonight. I am interested to see if he shows up."

"What did you say the meeting is about?"

"Simply to have a drink."

***

Daniel Wright stared outside of his hotel window and watched as the rain fell from the sky. He wondered if the other members of the group have decided he was too untrustworthy to keep on the team. There was a high chance he would be walking to his death tonight. He has known these men for a long time, and they have never once just met for drinks and drinks alone.

Grabbing an umbrella before he went, he nodded his head to the doorman as he walked outside of the hotel. Tonight he wanted to walk and let the dying embers of disappointment and rage burn out of him.

The moon was only half full tonight. The scent of rain heavy in the air; unfortunately, the trace of car fumes was also present and even the rain could not wash that scent away.

They were foolish to think that the orders given could not be traced. And to think that the people they were killing have no meaning in life, that they were just a statistic. The deceit of what they were doing revolted him.

His own fellow Americans he worked with have plunged him into this abyss of deceit, one from which there was no return. How in God's name could this have happened? How could they have let it happen?

Regrettably, it has happened. Little did they know that he has written down the facts. Not only has he done that, but in the event of his death, he has instructed his attorney to send everything to the CDC and all the main news channels. His death and the deaths from the vaccine would not be in vain.

The revulsion of what they have done would be known worldwide by everyone. The nation would soon know just how undemocratic their President was.

This project, which had been so carefully thought out, has become a ticking time bomb. No one truly comprehended how serious the repercussions would be. He knew the end of their long and distinguished careers was what waited for him and those participating in this project.

***

Kevin looked down at his watch and wondered where in the hell Daniel was. The man was more than fifteen minutes late. As if sensing his growing uneasiness, Thompson stated, "Daniel has forsaken us. He is more than likely right now talking to a newscaster about this story."

Shaking his head, Kevin stated, "No, he isn't that stupid. His own career would be ruined."

"We must do something about him."

Kevin nodded his head in agreement. Before they could continue their conversation, though, Daniel walked up to the table. "Sorry I am late, but it is raining harder than I thought."

Thompson looked at the man astonished, "You walked here in this weather?"

"I needed to clear my head." Before he continued with the conversation, the waitress arrived.

"Sir, can I get you something to drink?"

Without hesitation, Daniel ordered. "Scotch and water. Easy on the ice."

In no time, Daniel had his drink in front of him. He downed it in one swallow and motioned for the waitress to bring him another.

Thompson smiled over at Daniel; his expression barely hiding the contempt he felt for him. "Where have you been lately? I have been trying to catch up with you."

Daniel looked over at him and answered, "I do have regular work to do as well. My constituents want to see me working, especially if I want to be reelected."

"Well then Daniel Winters, have any of your fellow members of Congress said anything about the budget?"

Taking another sip of his scotch, Daniel shook his head. "No, they are all busy trying to work on their own version of how to reduce spending."

Thompson tried to calm Daniel's nerves. "You have nothing to worry about. Once the order came through to begin the vaccine, it was as if the direct order came from God. We are completely covered on our end; besides, no one has even the faintest idea of what has been planned."

"If the CDC does obtain a sample of blood, are we certain that they will not be able to tell that the virus actually came from the vaccine?"

Kevin shook his head. "There will be no way to trace how the virus was transmitted. It dies almost as soon as it enters the body and leaves behind nothing but destruction."

Daniel closed his eyes as the horror of what they have started flashed through his mind once more. He wished he was never considered for this group. As Secretary of Defense, you must be tough as nails and he always considered himself a ruthless player, but this... this was not what he signed up for.

Chapter 8

Wilson Pierron went to bed last night with a sore throat, and this morning he was having extreme difficulty breathing along with a fever of 106.

He could hear the doctor talking, but found it hard to concentrate on what he was saying. Thankfully, his son came over this morning to check on him. He hated to think of what may have happened had his son not shown up.

He found this whole ordeal frightening. He could not think of a time when he was this sick. Not only was he having a hard time catching his breath, but he felt as if his insides were literally cooking from the high fever.

He felt someone take a hold of his hand. "Dad, how are you doing?"

Brad Pierron has never met a doctor more empathetic to his patients than his dad's current doctor. For an Emergency Room physician, he actually listened to how his dad was feeling, but he also seemed to care.

Dr. Johnson looked over at the son, "Your dad needs to be admitted into the hospital for a few days. We are waiting on the blood test results, but I am fairly certain he does indeed have the flu."

Letting out a deep sigh Brad replied, "But I don't understand; Dad just had his flu shot."

"It is more than likely that your dad already had the flu. We are seeing that a lot this season."

Chapter 9

Inside Air Force One, President Edwards listened to the various news reports regarding the virus. He has been in meetings for two days now and hasn't had a chance to even think about what was going on in his own country.

With every stop he made, he came face to face with the repudiation of his presidency. He was constantly criticized, all because he has not been able to balance the budget for the last four years. What made him think this time around he could? He was frustrated that no one could see what he has done for this country; instead, all they did was focus on the negative.

There was so much hate for him suddenly, and the remnants of hate kept replaying in his mind. When did his popularity change? The public couldn't see that he was trying his best. Hell, they kept looking at Congress to solve their problems. In his opinion, most of them were incompetent, with shit for brains.

Most of them have served more than two consecutive terms and none have been able to solve the country's budget problems. Thanks to them, and the previous presidents, this country has gone to hell in a hand basket.

Even with his popularity falling, he remained committed to making this a better country. He planned on proving to those doubting him that his second term would not turn out badly, unlike other presidents.

He would meet the blistering attacks head on and show them that he would balance the budget, where no other president had been able to. He would show them that he could clear the deficit they were in. No one else fully understood the dichotomy of his job. It takes a very strong man to not be destroyed by what others think of you and to rise above hatred.

He was lost in his thoughts when a text came through as they landed. "We need to talk."

***

President Edwards decided to hold the clandestine meeting in the Presidential living quarters rather than meeting somewhere else. At this late hour, no one would even take particular notice of his guest.

Kevin Jameson found the President in an overstuffed chair with a roaring fire in the fireplace. In one hand, he held a glass of scotch and the other, a fine cigar. He was kicked back in his smoking jacket and comfortable shoes. For a moment, the President's relaxed stance annoyed Kevin with all that was going on right now.

Kevin went over and poured himself a glass of scotch and sat on the couch. He waited for the President to signal that he was ready to discuss the matter. "What is so important that you felt you must see me immediately rather than just talk via phone?" President Edwards asked.

Kevin only showed stress in the way he rolled the scotch in the glass. "We have a problem with Daniel Wright."

"Then I suggest you take care of it."

***

Down the hall in a small hidden room, Bill Kingsley sat in front of a battery of closed circuit television screens closely monitoring the meeting. No one except a select few knew of this room, not even the President of the United States.

As he listened to the conversation taking place, he became increasingly concerned. For now, he allowed the President to believe he was the one in control and that no one, including Bill, knew the existence of this group and project. As director of the Central Intelligence Agency, it had been so easy to convince the President that this was in the best interest of the United States. After all, he was the principal intelligence advisor to the President and who would know better than him. Since it was also Bill's duty to coordinate intelligence activities between different agencies within the United States Government, he knew just which people were needed for this special group.

Picking up the phone, he called Thompson, "Did you know that Jameson was meeting with the President tonight?"

Thompson let out a low curse under this breath. "No. I assumed the only one we had to watch out for was Daniel Wright."

"Well, Jameson is telling the President about his own concerns with regards to Daniel Wright. I thought we were taking care of this ourselves."

"So did I, sir. I will make sure that Daniel Wright is taken care of and I will keep a close eye on Jameson as well."

"We have too much at stake for anything to go wrong."

Chapter 10

It took every bit of her strength, but Lynette Grant managed to sit up in bed. Her stomach was still queasy and it has become a struggle to breathe, but she was sitting up.

Why did she listen to her neighbor? She never got a flu shot. She should have told Eileen that she did not want or need the shot. Instead, Eileen convinced her to accompany her, as well as get the shot. This year the shots were free and living on such a tight income as she did, free was the best motivator. Not long after getting the flu vaccine, her hands and feet were swollen and she had difficulty breathing as well.

Lynette cursed softly as another wave of nausea hit her. She was supposed to go to church with Eileen this morning, but she couldn't even find the strength to get out of bed, much less get herself dressed.

As she moved to pick up the phone to call Eileen, her body was seized with a violent coughing attack. She could actually hear the liquid moving around in her chest.

As the gurgling noise persisted, she began to panic. She gasped for air as sweat poured down her forehead, stinging her eyes. She now doubted her decision to obtain the flu shot. It was supposed to prevent you from coming down with the flu, instead now she seemed to have come down with a horrible case.

Could it be just a coincidence that she felt bad the day after receiving the shot? She must have already been infected with the virus before getting the flu shot. After all, her grandkids had visited the other day and Brenda mentioned that Evan had woken up with the sniffles, which was why he didn't come with his brother and sister.

As she reached for the phone again, another coughing spasm attacked her body. She felt as if she was actually drowning from the fluid building up in her chest. She needed help quickly, before she actually drowned to death. She should call 911.

As she sat up a little more, she caught a glimpse of herself in the dresser mirror. She scared even herself when she saw her image. Her face was ashen, her hair matted with sweat.

Before reaching for the phone one last time, a sudden stabbing pain resonated through her head. Her consciousness wavered, before everything around her went black.

Chapter 11

Dr. Ray Johnson has only worked at St. Anne General Hospital in Springport, Louisiana for nine months, but he was impressed with its modern upgrades. Unlike the last hospital he worked in, St. Anne's managed to keep their technology up to date.

 "Dr. Johnson you are needed in the Emergency Room, STAT!" He heard the announcement over the intercom.

He worked rotation in the Emergency Room. Ever since realizing he wanted to be a doctor, he also knew that he wanted to work in the ER. It seemed to be the place where all the action was and he was correct in his assumption.

He preferred the night shift, as they seemed to always be the wildest. At this hour, there were no urgent care centers open, so he treated a variety of patients seeking medical help. On any night, he could see patients with gunshot wounds, stabbings, broken bones, to the gravely ill.

It was going on one o'clock in the morning and so far this was a slow night for him. He has already admitted a woman to Cardiology for a heart attack and treated a broken leg from a head on collision.

But thankfully, he had time to catch up on his discharge summaries, which was always a blessing. Paperwork was his least favorite thing to do, but a necessity.

Dr. Johnson looked at the elderly woman lying on the exam room table and asked, "Where did she come from?"

Nurse Sally Hanson replied, "Her neighbor became worried when she hadn't seen her in a few days. When she didn't answer her phone, the neighbor called the police and they called the ambulance."

She informed Dr. Johnson, "The neighbor told the paramedics that she had taken Mrs. Mable Guillory to the clinic just the other day for her flu vaccine. Later that afternoon when the neighbor checked on Mrs. Guillory, she mentioned that she didn't feel well and was going to lie down."

Dr. Johnson looked over the patient's chart. She appeared to be extremely dehydrated and running a high fever. "Let's get her sedated and up to a room. It will be best to admit her due to her age. It appears that she didn't receive her flu vaccine in time."

As Dr. Johnson hung up the chart on the bed, he instructed, "Please let me know if her condition worsens."

As he headed to his office, he was called once more to the emergency room; there was another potential flu patient. If this kept up, it would be a very long night. He hoped that he would at least be able to take a nap on his sofa, but it seemed sleep may be a long time coming for him.

Chapter 12

Carlos Ramirez approached the tee box of the eighth hole, when a brawny stranger walked up to him. With it being such a beautiful day and not wanting to worry about his strokes, he allowed the man to play through.

The stranger shook his head, "I can wait. I am in no hurry."

Carlos smiled at him and said in his heavy, strong Mexican accent, "No please, I insist. I am in no hurry."

Extending his hand, the stranger said, "Thanks, man."

Carlos never felt the prick in his hand, until it was too late, "What the…"

As quickly as he appeared, the man disappeared. Almost as if he was nothing more than a ghost.

***

As Thompson drove away from the golf course, an evil, sadistic smile formed on his face. When the drug lord who has given the CIA problems over recent years dropped dead, no one would even think of conspiracy. He would have died of nothing more than a bad strain of the flu. It had been too easy to get to Carlos here. The drug lord kept his same golf date and never had protection with him. He truly believed he was unreachable. They were able to reach him and this would show him, but it would be too late for Carlos.

Now, it was time to move onto the next phase of the plan. There were many more that needed to be reached before the flu season was over.

***

Two hours later, Carlos Ramirez died at the bar in the prestigious golf course's clubhouse. As his body was loaded onto the gurney, everyone there stared at the sheet lined corpse.

As the paramedics brought the body to the morgue, they discussed the possibility that this man could have possibly infected everyone in that clubhouse with whatever killed him. The very thought brought chills to the medics.

Those who saw Mr. Ramirez earlier stated that he seemed fine when he came in, but by the time he finished his round of golf, he looked as if he aged twenty years. The members also stated that the man coughed his way through the place; not caring about whom he coughed on either.

At the morgue, the medical examiner was told about the witnesses' statements, just in case it turned out that whatever killed him was contagious. The paramedics also gave him a list containing all of those who were present at the time of his death, in case they needed to make notifications.

Chapter 13

Olivia Landry pulled the afghan she made years ago over her tired old body and curled up on the couch. The living room furniture was overstuffed in deep mahogany leather that called to her as soon as she saw it. As she settled into the couch, there was an instant feeling of familiarity as the cushioned padding tailored to the contours of her body.

Several hours later, Olivia found herself extremely cold and shivering, despite the warmth of the house. As she tried to get up, her body broke out in a cold sweat. From the aching in her body, she knew she had the flu. Why didn't she listen to her daughter, Anna Marie, and go last week for the flu shot instead of waiting until yesterday?

Through clenched teeth, she forced herself up from the couch as deep pain wracked her body. Every muscle in her body hurt.

She hobbled to the kitchen. Every step and every movement that she made caused an explosion of pain down her back and through her legs. She called her daughter, "I think I need to go to the hospital."

***

As the gurney wheeled Olivia down the corridors into the exam room, she watched as the overhead lights appeared to zip by. The lights seemed to hypnotize her.

As the nurses poked and prodded her, she slipped in and out of consciousness. She remembered them saying something about needing to rehydrate her. She lost count of the number of nurses who took her pulse, temperature, and blood pressure.

As she slipped into unconsciousness, she noticed a strange odor underneath the crisp, clean smell of the hospital. It was something she had smelled before, but she couldn't seem to recall where she had smelled it.

Olivia Landry's family gathered in her room, all fearing that their mother was close to death. The doctor informed them, "We have drawn blood and run a viral antigen test. By all accounts, your mother has a normal strain of influenza; unfortunately, the antibiotics do not seem to be working." Dr. Johnson looked over at the daughter, "Are you certain that when she received the vaccine yesterday she had no symptoms of the flu?"

Anna Marie shook her head, "She was fine. She was complaining of feeling achy yesterday after her vaccine, but the nurse explained that it was common."

Dr. Johnson scratched his head, "She must have already contracted the flu before her vaccine."

"But she looked fine."

Dr. Johnson looked at the family with sympathy showing in his eyes. "I am so sorry. We will continue pumping her with antibiotics."

Olivia could hear the doctor talking to her family. She could hear the sadness in her daughter's voice.

The doctor didn't expect her to live through this, but he was wrong. She wasn't ready to die. She may be old, but soon, she would welcome her first great grandchild into this world and there was no way she would miss that.

If only she wasn't so tired and weak, she would tell them so herself. If only her body would listen to her mind's commands.

Suddenly, her breathing became shallow. Her body cried out for oxygen.

Instinct alone told her that death was fast approaching. Her life began to flash through her mind. It was almost as if she was watching it play out on an old black and white screen. She could see herself as a small child and then the pictures turned vivid. She was walking down the aisle to her soon to be husband; how she missed staring into those dark eyes of his. They always reminded her of a warm cup of coffee. Soon, she would join him in heaven.

They had such a wonderful life. He dreamed of traveling to exotic ports as a sailor, but instead, he settled down and married her. She often wondered if he regretted marrying her instead of traveling the world. He never said anything while he was alive, but with her own death near, she started regretting certain mistakes in her own life.

A cooling sensation moved through her veins, as the pain she experienced suddenly disappeared. For once in the last few days, she finally felt good. Could it be that the antibiotics were working? A voice called out to her from somewhere in the room. It was her husband. With a final gurgling noise, death took her body. As she took her husband's hand in hers, she welcomed death.

Chapter 14

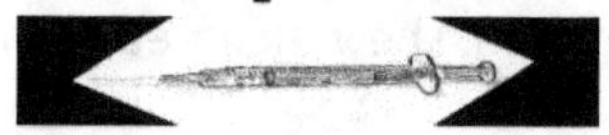

Amanda Bowers applied her eyeliner with expert precision. Her steel gray eyes were in stark contrast to her auburn hair, giving her an alluring quality. Her thick hair has a natural wave, which tended to frizz in the summer heat. She pulled her hair back in a tight bun, which helped to accentuate her high cheekbones and striking eyes.

She has only been in her new position with the Center for Disease Control for about six months now, but she enjoyed every minute of her job. She thrived on the relentless pressure that came with the role. The only negative aspect of her job was all the paperwork that came with the position. At least once a week, she looked over the CDC's morbidity and mortality report to see if there were any rash outbreaks of food borne illnesses and other diseases. The pressure and bureaucracy grew every day.

The thought of a new strain of a virus to examine excited her immensely. She didn't even mind being on call at all hours, meetings, deadlines, and spreadsheets.

In her opinion, it was an honor to work for the CDC. They had so many successes in the past, and now, she was part of that very team. There was something satisfying about being a medical detective. This was what she studied and trained for. Her department was at the forefront of research. In the past, virology played second fiddle to bacteriology; however, now virology was where all the action was.

Currently, they were waiting for blood work from several deaths, which may have ensued from a new virus strain. She could hardly wait for the samples to arrive. It was just unfortunate that there have been so many deaths as a result of this virus.

By the time Amanda made it into the office that morning, it was almost nine o'clock. Henry, the security guard, sat crookedly on his metal stool. She was astonished to see that Henry was still working, but for a man close to seventy, he looked good for his age.

She smiled over at him and waved. He gave her a tired wave back, "Good morning, Henry."

"How are you doing, Dr. Bowers?"

"I'm fine, Henry. You look as if you don't feel well, though."

"Oh, it is just a touch of a cold I am sure. Went to the clinic the other day and got my flu shot."

"Henry, you could have gotten the vaccine here!"

Waving his hands at her, "My wife and I went to the clinic this year for our free shots. This is the first time the government has ever offered them for free."

"Well, take care, Henry."

Before heading to her office, Amanda stopped by her secretary's desk. "Jane, do you know if any of the labs arrived yet?"

Jane shook her head. "No, not yet. I called several of the hospitals and they all assured me that they were sent. I am not sure what the holdup is."

Amanda let out a sigh. "I was hoping to have some answers today. Please see if they possibly have tracking numbers for the packages?"

"I am already on it." Jane shifted in her seat, "I know this may sound strange, but by chance, did you send some field agents to hospitals to pick up samples?"

"You know better than that. We have all been told the importance of keeping unnecessary expenses down."

Jane looked up at her boss, "Well, I know I didn't, but I did have a few hospitals inform me they gave their labs to someone from the CDC."

Amanda yelled, "What! That can't be right. We need to find out who would have ordered this. I swear if Infectious Diseases is making a peremptory jump on this before we are ready, I will scream. That man can be so impatient at times."

Chapter 15

Dr. Johnson, the other doctors, and nurses at St. Anne General Hospital, sat in the conference room while the administrator, Bill Gaudet, paced back and forth. Bill was normally a cool and composed man, but the strain of what was happening here these last few days was wearing on him.

"There is no doubt that we need to keep the patients contained, or the whole hospital will be infected."

Dr. Adams asked, "What about the Pandemic Response Protocol established by the CDC?"

Bill ran his hands through his hair. "As we have found out, that all looks good on paper, but when it is time to actually put the wheels in motion, what looks good on paper doesn't always work." As he peered outside before explaining, "A triage is being set up in the emergency room. No one will be permitted through those doors until it has been confirmed whether or not they do indeed have this particular strain of virus. A floor has been dedicated to those infected with it and an elevator has been designated for those patients only."

Dr. Johnson asked, "Are other hospitals using this same protocol?"

"Yes. The smaller hospitals will have the patients confirmed with the virus sent to our facility. They in return are going to allow us to send patients seeking minor medical care to their facilities. They just don't have the space to quarantine these patients." Bill looked at those sitting around him before adding, "I must warn you that there are always unknown variables. We just don't have any idea how large this could be or how many more we can expect to die."

Dr. Adams asked, "Do we have any information on the virus? Where it came from?"

Bill shook his head, "So far, we have been given no information. The first tests showed that it was simply a virus, but a deadly one. We have no idea how the patients contracted the virus, but we do know it was not airborne. So far, others who have come in contact with the patients did not contract the virus. From what we can tell, it spreads quickly and there is no cure at this time. Samples have been sent to the CDC, but they have stated it could be a while before the strain is identified."

Dr. Johnson stated, "So basically, the only thing we do know is that we are dealing with a deadly, fast spreading virus. The patients present with a high fever and severe cough. The virus seems to attack the respiratory system first, before compromising the entire system. In several patients, it is only a matter of hours before the disease spreads throughout the entire body."

Dr. Adams replied, "If only we had time to observe these patients. This damn disease isn't giving us time to properly evaluate it. I have been practicing medicine for almost thirty years and I have never seen anything like this."

Bill cleared his throat, "I want to keep this as low key as possible right now. As Dr. Adams stated, the public will start to panic when they find out. The less that is in the media at this time, the better off we are. If a reporter tries to talk with you, forward them to my office. I will have the Press Relations Department work on this."

Bill reminded the doctors, "We need to keep a close eye on the people who had direct contact with the ill and deceased."

Chapter 16

Dr. Amanda Bowers just made it home, when her phone rang, "Dr. Bowers?" asked the CDC duty officer.

"Yes."

"This is your lucky day. There is an epidemic in Springport, Louisiana. Dr. Roy Johnson requested our help. There appears to be several deaths resulting from a flu strain down there. A flight reservation and hotel accommodations have been arranged. I don't anticipate that you will be there for long, though. Once you have determined that it is a simple viral outbreak, you will be shipped back home."

***

By the time Amanda retrieved her suitcase from the baggage carousel and rented a car, the sun was starting to rise.

She headed to the hospital, since if the cases appeared to be nothing more than a simple flu, she would not need a hotel room anyway. Her instructions were to return back to the CDC as soon as possible, as other areas were already calling in requesting their help as well. She asked for a busy season and it appeared that was just what she was getting.

The hospital was small compared to Atlanta standards. As she got out of the car, she stretched before retrieving her briefcase. She made sure to include a note pad, pens, pencils, and a current textbook on domestic virology.

Once inside the hospital, Amanda was greeted with the smell of disinfectant. She instantly felt at home here. At the information booth, she introduced herself, "I am Dr. Amanda Bowers with the CDC."

The nurse looked up to see a young doctor standing in front of her. "Dr. Johnson is the one who called you. You just missed him, but Dr. Adams was briefed as well as the hospital administrator." Over the PA system the nurse called for Mr. Bill Gaudet.

As Amanda waited for the hospital administrator, she looked over the emergency room. For a supposed epidemic to be hitting here, the emergency room was rather quiet. She had expected to see lines of people, not just a few sitting sporadically through the room.

The nurse interrupted her thoughts, "Can I get you some coffee?"

"That would be nice. Thank you."

A striking man walked off the elevator and headed right for Amanda. "Dr. Bowers, thank you for coming so quickly. I'm the administrator, Bill Gaudet, I called Dr. Johnson to let him knew that you arrived."

 "It's nice to meet you, but if you don't mind, I would rather jump right in."

As Bill Gaudet led the way to the floor where they had isolated the patients, she asked, "How many patients have been diagnosed with this strain of the flu?"

"It is not the number of sick that has us worried, but the fatality rate."

"What is the fatality rate?"

Gaudet ran his hand through his hair, "As of this morning, the hospital admitted fifteen and of those admitted, ten have passed away. The five that remain are on death's door as we speak."

As they were talking, Bill received a text message. "I stand corrected; two more were admitted just now."

"With a city the size of Springport, though, those numbers can't be too high?"

Shaking his head, he replied, "No, I suppose not, but what is worrisome is the fact that nothing we do seems to help the patients."

"What are the demographics of these patients?"

"So far, ninety nine percent of the patients are elderly. We had a few younger patients come in, but they were what could be considered high risk patients. One has a compromised immune system from a recent fight with cancer and another has, or I should say had, rheumatoid arthritis."

As Amanda listened to all of Bill's concerns, she soon realized that she did not have the power to immediately assist this poor hospital. While it did warrant concern, because of the strict budget cuts they were under, it would have to fall under the local government's control and not hers. She hated breaking news to hospital and medical care providers that were hoping the CDC would come in like a knight on a white horse to save the day.

Before she made the final decision, though, she must obtain some basic information, which would be helpful in her decision making. She needed to look at the cultures to see if this was a new virus. Next, she had to determine if a problem did really exist; she would need rudimentary statistics for that. If she could characterize the illness and make a specific diagnosis, the next step would be to determine host factors. She would need to determine the time, place, and circumstances of each patient in order to find out what they had in common. Then, the next question was the transmission of the illness. It was imperative that she determined if this was an infectious agent and just how it was spread.

As if reading her mind, Bill informed her, "All the patients have had a positive diagnosis of influenza, but when you look at it under a microscope, you can see a few small differences. It is almost as if the genes were altered in some way."

"Do you have an idea on the time frame from the onset of symptoms to hospitalization?"

Bill led her into one of the patient's rooms. "I believe that you should see the patients first."

Amanda would humor the man for now, but she was certain that seeing the patients at this juncture would accomplish nothing. As he made the introductions, Amanda looked over the patient. Interrupting her thoughts, Bill continued on, "All the patients were isolated to this floor. We keep them separated according to the progression of the disease. Right now, they are being kept in rooms, but there is a chance that we may have to transform the ICU ward to care for these patients. Currently though, we have enough private rooms to treat them."

Amanda removed the patient's chart from his bed and looked over his vital signs. His temperature was steadily rising, with no help from the antibiotics that were being pumped into his body. "It appears that this particular strain of virus is resilient to antibiotics."

"That is our fear as well."

Just from a simple review of the files, Amanda was certain that the patients were receiving superb care. The lab work and various other tests were exhaustive. The doctors here were doing just what the CDC would do in this current situation.

With a grim expression, she told him, "I am terribly sorry, but at this time, I just don't see where the CDC can step in." She could see the hurt in his eyes. She quickly said a few words to encourage him, "You are following all the right protocols here. The only thing I would suggest is that you place a barrier up so that in case it does turn communicable, the disease will be contained to just this floor."

"You are right. I warned Dr. Johnson that it is too early to call in the CDC."

Handing him her business card she said, "Please call me if any more problems arise. I will keep you apprised of any new developments that I learn as well; unfortunately, until the situation worsens here, there is nothing I can do. To be honest with you, I believe the only reason I was sent here is to placate you.”

Nodding his head, he agreed, “I understand that of course. I was just hoping for a little more insight.”

“Would it be possible to have a copy of the patients’ charts and a sample of their blood work sent to the CDC?” She explained further, “I would take the samples with me, but I am on a commercial flight and with the current protocols in place, it has become difficult to carry items back with us.”

“Of course, that won’t be a problem. I already had copies of the charts made for you to review and as far as the samples, I will have those rushed to the CDC.”

Shaking his hand, she said, “Thank you so much. I hope that this turns out to be nothing more than a fluke and that the deaths will stop.” Even as Amanda said the words, she knew that there was little to no truth to her presumption. In all honestly, she looked for the numbers to steadily increase.

***

On the plane, she pulled out the patients’ charts to review. Other than the same symptoms, the only commonality she could find was they all received the flu vaccine right before they started showing symptoms. That fact had her a little concerned; the vaccine was supposed to prevent the flu not aggravate symptoms.

To make her report easier to write up, she started listing every bit of information that could possibly have significance, including the fact that all the patients received the flu vaccine prior to the onset of symptoms. She kept telling herself that this wasn't significant, but a little voice in the back of her head kept telling her that it was an important fact.

Of course, it could just be coincidental that the symptoms presented themselves at the same time as the inoculation. Some could even take a week before they presented themselves.

Amanda kept going through all the charts and recording her findings in the notebook. Reading the charts also gave her a clearer clinical picture of just what they were dealing with. So far, all the patients presented with the same symptoms; headache, chills, high fever, muscle pain, stomach cramps, sore throat, and a terrible cough.

As she collected her baggage in Atlanta, her phone rang. It was her direct supervisor and the man who hired her, Dr. George Bentley. "How was your first field assignment?"

Letting out a tired sigh she answered, "Depressing. I don't think the hospital administrator took it well that there was nothing we could do to help. I have all the patient records and will write up my report tonight, but at this time, it presents as unfortunate deaths related to influenza."

"Was there anything to show that this will be an epidemic on our hands?"

"No. There is some genetic modification, but nothing of significance can be noted. I asked that samples of the blood work be sent to the CDC just so we can do more testing, but to be honest, I don't see where we are needed."

He quickly agreed, "You did good. You were correct in your assumption. They will have to rely on the local government to help out. If it spreads or worsens, we can step in, but not until then. Several more areas have called in with the same diagnosis, so it is something that will need to be closely monitored, but that is all at this time."

Amanda grimly stated, "It is just so overwhelming. These people are dying; yet, there is nothing I can do about it."

"Amanda, you have to remind yourself that as an epidemiologist you look at data differently than the treating doctors. You have to look at the whole picture, where they are looking at the patient."

"I understand that," she replied, "I'm on my way back to the office, I will talk with you there."

***

Once she made it back to the office, Dr. Bentley called her into his office. "You look tired."

"Just jet lag."

"Well, let's go down to the cafeteria and I will buy you a cup of coffee. You can tell me about your exciting visit while we are down there."

Since it was already mid-afternoon, the cafeteria was pretty much vacant. They sat at a window overlooking the courtyard. "I know you feel guilty about not being able to do more at the hospital, but you did a superb job handling yourself. You would think that you were an experienced veteran at this."

"I just wish I could find out where the virus originated from is all. This particular strain is different from the other patients. It was almost as if it mutated." She replied.

Bentley took her hand in his, "There have been times when the CDC was unable to trace a virus. It is devastating, but it happens. From what we can tell, this virus dies out fast, which is good news. Yes, the bad news is that it kills the host, but at least it dies out before it can be passed onto another victim." Looking her directly in the eyes he added, "You are being much too hard on yourself."

"But we do not know how these patients were infected or why everyone who comes in contact with this particular virus dies. I have a feeling this particular virus will keep popping up." Amanda saw how devastating the virus could be to the elderly and high risk patients. She shuddered in fear, thinking of the numbers they may be dealing with.

Chapter 17

Across from the White House, in a hidden office in the basement of the Old Executive Office Building, four men meet to discuss the development of their project. With all that was going on, none of them wanted to take a chance of being seen together in public.

Their leader ordered the massacre and now they were bound together by this very order. Each of these men discovered something about themselves that he wouldn't have believed possible. Thompson discovered that he liked being in control of death. He felt almost like a grim reaper.

Now, he would do everything in his power to protect them all from liberal do-gooders who have taken over their nation. He would not let someone else make the decisions with regard to his future. He discovered that access was power and he had the access to do what he wanted.

Yes, by moving behind the scenes they ensured that those whom they trusted filled the needed positions in government and elsewhere.

Thompson was the only one in this group, though, that knew there was actually someone else higher in their chain of command. This man controlled things in secret.

This project had indeed been the leader's idea. He simply put a bug in the President's ear, which he took hook, line, and sinker.

Daniel asked, "So, are we certain that no one has any clue as to what is truly going on?"

Kevin nodded his head, 'So far, everything is going as planned; however, this Amanda Bowers, with the CDC, is one smart cookie. So far, she refuses to listen to reason and is still intent on pursuing her investigation of the fatalities."

Daniel let out a curse. "Son of a bitch. I thought we had all of the agencies under control."

Kevin tried to calm the man down, "Don't worry. We are keeping a close eye on her. So far, we have prevented any samples from being delivered to her."

Thompson reminded Kevin, "Just remember, if you do decide to eliminate her, it must look like an accident. The last thing we need is a murder investigation to bring even more attention to these fatalities. I am certain that if a member of the CDC is murdered right now, there will be no containing the press. They will see a conspiracy and immediately run with it."

Kevin nodded his head, "Don't worry, whatever I do will look like an accident. The last thing I want is linkage."

Kevin began to hand out the reports they had so far. "Here are the preliminary reports of everyone who has been given the vaccine and their deaths."

President Edwards smiled at the reports. "These are marvelous, if I may say so. In only a short amount of time, it looks as if several areas have been inoculated and we are already seeing results."

Kevin stated, "The Department of Health is helping to keep the panic down. They are on board with promoting the importance of the vaccine."

Once the reports were read, they were shredded. President Edwards looked at Kevin, "We are certain that there is no proof of what we have done? The last thing we need is someone sending any proof that they have to the press."

Kevin simply replied, "Everything is under control. You have nothing to worry about, sir. This administration, or group for that matter, will not be brought down by betrayal."

Chapter 18

Karen Davis picked up the phone and tried to call her father once more. For the last several months, she and her husband, Jeff, have tried to convince her dad to come live with them. Every time they asked, he refused, not wanting to leave the house where he spent most of his life.

Karen felt that it had more to do with the fact that she now lived in Virginia, far away from Louisiana; her dad would not be able to visit her mom's grave. Karen's mother died from breast cancer almost six years ago now and her poor father still had not gotten over her death.

Looking over at her husband, she said, "He's still not answering."

Jeff quietly asked, "Why don't you call your cousin, Mark? With him being a paramedic, he can make sure your dad is doing better."

As she dialed Mark's number, Jeff reminded her, "Be sure to tell Mark that the last time you spoke to him he wasn't feeling too well."

"Mark, it's Karen."

"Hey Karen. I'd love to talk to you a little more, but I am just starting my shift."

"Mark, I'm really sorry to bother you, but this is kind of important. I haven't been able to get in touch with Dad.

The last time I spoke to him, he had just received a flu vaccine and wasn't feeling well."

"Let me get situated and then we will go check on Uncle Allan." Mark replied.

"Thank you so much, Mark."

****

Mark looked over at his partner, "Christine, before any calls come in, let's do a wellness check."

Christine let out a long sigh, "Let the police do the wellness check. I haven't even had a cup of coffee."

Mark pulled her over to the ambulance. "Come on. I'll buy you a cup of coffee on the way back. I know the man; he is my uncle."

"*Mon ami*, I am sorry."

Mark shrugged his shoulders, "My cousin is possibly worrying over nothing. The old man is undoubtedly out in his garden, where he is every day, and just didn't pay attention to the time of day."

It only took a few minutes to reach Allan Cheramie's house. At the front door, Mark knocked as loud as he could. The last time he stopped by to visit, his uncle could barely hear the doorbell.

Mark's next knock was louder. "Uncle Allan? Uncle Allan? It's Mark, Mark Cheramie. Karen called concerned about you." Calling out louder he said, "Come on, Uncle Allan, open up."

Mark looked over at Christine. "Did you see him out back in the garden?"

Christine shook her head and replied, "It looks as if the garden hasn't been tended to for a day or two. There are some vegetables out there that seem to be ripe for the picking."

Mark commented, "That doesn't sound like Uncle Allan. He usually picks vegetables in the morning and evening. I think it not only gives him something to do, but a reason to visit people. He is always bringing my mom a large bag of some sort of vegetable he raised."

Almost banging down the door this time he yells out, "Come on, Uncle Allan." Not receiving any sort of reply, Mark told Christine, "I think he usually keeps a spare key under one of the flower pots here on the porch." Mark found it under the third pot they looked under, "Got it!"

As soon as they walked into his uncle's home, the fetid smell of human waste greeted them. Christine told Mark, "I don't like this. Maybe, we should call the cops."

Mark moved deeper into the house and informed her, "He is laying on the couch." At the sight in front of him, Mark was paranoid that he would find his uncle deceased. He was covered in his own excrement and his eyes were wide open, staring right at him.

Without warning, his Uncle Allan sat up abruptly and started to pull out his hair. Mark made his way over to his uncle, "Uncle Allan, it is me, Mark. I came to bring you to the hospital."

Instead of acknowledging his nephew, the old man continued to pull out his hair. Mark instructed Christine, "Get the fentanyl."

Christine opened her medical pack, removed the syringe, and quickly found a vein. Not long after injecting the elderly man with the medicine, his body went limp. Mark carefully laid his uncle back down on the couch. Christine suggested to Mark, "You better tell his daughter to get down here. He is burning up and doesn't look good at all."

"Let's get the stretcher and get him to the hospital. I will call Karen on the way over there."

Mark told Christine, "On three. One... two... three."

With complete ease, they lifted the stretcher into the ambulance. In one fluid movement, they pushed the frame forward into the shell housing and locked the sturdy legs in place.

As Dr. Johnson heard the call come in informing the hospital that the ambulance was bringing in another flu patient, he was not only concerned, but confused as well. It was normal during flu season to get several patients in the emergency room, but the numbers were higher than normal for the beginning of the season.

What concerned him was that several influenza patients had a strain of antigens in their blood that some of the others didn't. All of those with these particular antigens in their blood have passed away.

By the time the new patient was brought into the Emergency Room, he was unconscious. His rapid breathing appeared to be a strain on the elderly man's body.

The nurse exclaimed, "His temperature is 107 degrees; he is burning up with fever."

Just by looking at the patient, Dr. Johnson could tell he was cyanotic. His skin had a bluish tinge, which could only mean that the blood was not receiving enough oxygen. Even the poor man's nail beds were blue.

Dr. Johnson began a rushed, but thorough examination of the man. Taking out his stethoscope, as he has done thousands of times before, he listened for a heartbeat. Not only was the man's breathing rapid, but so was his heart rate. It was beating at twice the normal rate.

Calling out to the nurse he ordered, "We need an electrocardiogram and a chest film, stat! We also need to make sure the lab is rushing the blood tests. We need those now."

As the nurse hurried to carry out his orders, he completed the rest of the physical exam. There was no doubt in his mind that this man had the same fatal flu as the other patients.

When the nurse handed Dr. Johnson the labs, his fears were confirmed. The man's white blood count was 2000, well below the normal range of 5,000 to 10,000. His white blood cells were no longer able to fight the infection.

He also took notice of the "Blood Hemolysis" results. As with the other patients, something was destroying the red blood cells too rapidly in a very abnormal manner.

His hemoglobin count was 3.1 grams. The trace of oxygen in the blood was basically non-existent.

As with the other patients, his body continued to shut down, despite the administration of antibiotics, digitalis, and oxygen. Before Dr. Johnson could order another round of hydrocortisone, the alarms went off.

Dr. Johnson reached over and began turning off the machines one by one. Exactly forty minutes after being admitted into the hospital, the patient passed away.

Before leaving the room, Nurse Brady walked in with a fresh surgical gown, mask, and cap. He was surprised to see her there with the items, but he was more unnerved by the fear he could see in her eyes, "It looks as if it will be a busy night. We have four more cases just like this one in the ER."

With tears in her eyes, she went on, "We also just had a six year old boy come in dead on arrival."

Johnson shook his head, as he followed Nurse Brady into the ER. All of them have seen death before, but this was like nothing any of them have ever worked with.

On his way, he tried to think of something to say to help ease the fear the nurse was feeling, but his mind went blank. By the end of the night, all four patients were deceased and two more flu cases admitted as well. Only one patient had survived.

Dr. Johnson looked at his watch and saw that he only had one hour left of this nightmarish shift. Nurse Brady rushed over to him, "A policeman just called. They are bringing in a homeless man who was found wandering the streets. The arresting officer could feel the heat resonating off him."

Running his hands through his hair, he said, "I have never seen anything like this. Did we win some kind of lottery tonight?"

Instead of waiting for an answer, he began walking back to his office. There had to be a common denominator between all of these patients. He planned on pouring over their medical records once more to see if he could find out just what that was.

By the time he finished reading all of the medical charts on each patient, the only common denominator was they all had received their flu vaccinations right before their deaths. He couldn't help but think how cruel fate could be. He wondered if they had managed to get the vaccines a week before, would that have prevented their unfortunate deaths?

Chapter 19

Harold Morgan has always taken pride in his health. If truth be told, he felt a little superior to everyone else. He has never once smoked, taken drugs, or drank alcohol. He stayed away from eggs and bacon for breakfast, fatty pork, or anything fried. His belief was that you never desecrated a temple, and his body was his temple.

He watched his diet so harshly that it had been impossible to keep a steady girlfriend. No one wanted to worry with a man who inspected everything he put in his mouth or who brooded over nutritional charts.

Not only did he follow a strict diet, but he also had a rigorous exercise regimen. Every morning, he took a brisk walk for exactly forty-five minutes before heading off to the gym.

He took pride in the fact that not once in his adult life has he even been sick, that was until now. Now, he was sitting in the emergency room waiting to be seen by a physician.

He just couldn't seem to understand how this happened. He had personal policies in place to keep this very thing from happening. He avoided anyone who had a cough or sneeze. He wore surgical gloves out in public, in order not to pick up any germs that may be waiting to enter his body. He washed his hands religiously; plus, he used hand sanitizers every chance he got. He even went as far as avoiding public restrooms; they were nothing more than a cesspool of germs waiting to enter the human body and cause illness.

The sore throat was what he first noticed, and by the time he stumbled into bed, he had a fever. Now, his head felt like it would explode at any moment and his throat was on fire.

Not wanting to go to the hospital, he tried soaking in a cool tub of water. That did little to help his rising fever. By the time he checked into the emergency room, his temperature was 105 degrees. He would be lucky if he didn't somehow manage to fry a few brain cells in the process.

When he was told that he had the flu, it made no sense to him. As always, he had his flu shot; he even sweet talked the young nurse into giving him one of the free flu shots the clinic was handing out to several of the other patients there. He may not be old enough for social security, but if the government was handing out freebies, he wanted in on it.

Chapter 20

The man walking through the hospital was tall and lithe. His black suit caught Nurse Sally Hanson's attention.

As he passed by her, he murmured a soft "Good evening," before moving on. For a moment, her breath caught in her throat. There was something intriguing about him, but at the same time something dangerous as well.

She watched as he moved down the hallway and disappeared, as he rounded a corner. Once he passed her, she wasn't able to recall anything in particular about his appearance, except his black suit. Strange how meeting some people there was nothing about their appearance that stayed with you, and others left distinct impressions that allowed you to remember specifics about them.

Dr. Johnson looked at the man dressed in black in front of him and feared that he may have stumbled on something more than he should have. In a very authoritative voice the man asked, "Dr. Johnson, just how long have you suspected that this was a new strain of a virus?"

"I suspected that it may be something more after the second patient was admitted into the hospital, but it wasn't until after the last few blood tests that I noticed the same antigens present in several of the patients. Unfortunately, all those patients are deceased. This virus spreads rapidly and I have had no luck curing any of the patients under my care."

He looked Dr. Johnson up and down before continuing, "What made you decide to contact the CDC?"

Dr. Johnson tried to place the man one more time. He looked more like CIA rather than the CDC. "There have been too many deaths. Was there a problem with me contacting the CDC? I am certain that I followed protocol."

Not wanting to alert the doctor the man quickly said, "No, no problem. I was just curious. Most of the doctors are blaming the cause of death due to their age and the fact that they have contracted the flu virus."

"If it had not been that they all seemed to come in at about the same time, I honestly may not have made a connection quite so early. It was as if there was an influx right from the start of the day and it was almost never ending. I have never seen anything like this, and when the labs all started coming in with the same antigens, I knew that we were dealing with a possibly very deadly strain of the flu."

"What did you do with the labs?"

Dr. Johnson replied, "We did just what the CDC requested. We prepared the lab samples for transport to the CDC. I believe the lab already sent the samples, but I can't be sure."

"I will go find out. I was sent to save you any unnecessary expenses; besides, they want to run their own tests as soon as possible to make sure that we are indeed not dealing with a deadly epidemic."

"Do you need me to show you where the lab is?" Before the man could answer, Dr. Johnson's phone rang. "I am sorry; it is the emergency room."

Waving his hands, he said, "I can find the lab. Besides, you are needed."

Dr. Johnson looked over the man once more; he was not sure where to place him. Something didn't sit right about him. He definitely didn't look like he would be a CDC errand boy.

Chapter 21

Douglas Richmond adjusted his glasses as he looked over the various newspaper articles on the table in front of him. He examined each article with equal attention in search of the next blog topic for his government conspiracy theories.

He liked working on his blog. It was the first productive thing he has done in a very long time. He discovered there were a bunch of people out there who believed in the same conspiracy theories as he did. It was great to connect with all of these various groups of people.

He considered writing about the rising cost of health care and how it was aimed at keeping the young people healthy, but silently eliminating the elderly from the earth, until the recent virus outbreak started. It was hard to argue that the elderly were of no concern to the government when they were offering free vaccines to the same people he claimed the government had no empathy for. The only thing he did find disturbing, however, was that these same people receiving the free vaccines were dying at an alarming rate.

Now, he had to find something else to blog about this week. With tens of thousands of followers, he had to keep them happy, if he wanted to keep them following.

As he glanced over the articles once more, he found an article in Sunday's paper that would be perfect for his blog and get people talking. It talked about how the U.S. government would send supplies and money to various nations around the world, but when an American city was stricken with an illness, the federal government left it up to the local governments to handle the problem. With everyone ill right now, it was the perfect conspiracy theory to work on.

If he played his cards right, this may draw even more followers to the site. His money mainly came from the ads displayed on the sides of the site page. The more people following him could result in the various ads on his site possibly being clicked, and each click earned him money.

When his alarm went off, it actually surprised him. Douglas was so busy reviewing all the articles that he didn't pay attention to the time. He only had a few minutes to get cleaned up and over to The Warehouse. He has been a bartender there for almost a year now. The pay was mediocre, but between the tips and girl's phone numbers he got, it was enough to keep him working there.

As he rushed out of the house, he was unaware of the black SUV sitting across the street from his house. He never heard the man falling in step behind him. All he felt was a stinging sensation when the man grabbed his shoulder. "Oh, sorry. I thought you were someone else."

He rubbed his shoulder and replied, "No problem, dude."

As the man turned back the other way, Douglas never even thought twice about the fact that his shoulder was throbbing, as if he were stung by something.

As Douglas made his way into the bar, he felt a slight tickle in the back of his throat. He pulled out a zinc lozenge from his pocket, hoping to ward off whatever it was he may be catching.

****

Douglas woke the next morning not feeling well at all. By mid-afternoon, he was considerably worse and actually considered calling in sick.

By five o'clock, though, he was incredibly ill and could barely stand up from lightheadedness. Never once did he consider he had the flu, because of his superior immune system, but there was a first time for everything.

His insides felt as if they were cooking; he had chills and a massive migraine headache. He sent Paul a text to let him knew that he would not be working tonight. His throat was on fire and he doubted he could even say the words over the phone.

In the middle of the night, violent stomach cramps wracked through his body. He attempted to drag himself to the bathroom, but he was so weak that he collapsed on the bedroom floor. He could not find the strength to even make it to the bathroom. He has never been this sick in all of his life.

He died there on the floor, lying in his own vomit. They had nothing to fear from him anymore. The CIA would no longer have to worry about what he talked about on his blog. He would no longer be able to instill fear in the general public about mass conspiracy theories.

Chapter 22

Kevin Jameson found himself in Atlanta, Georgia for yet another surveillance detail. He has come to abhor Atlanta; perhaps, it was the south altogether. He despised the people here, but more importantly, he detested the climate here. Even though it was winter, the temperature was not as cold as it was back home. His stomach clenched at just the mere thought of the heat and humidity that plagued the south in the summer.

Across from the building was a small café with plenty of windows overlooking the street. His stomach let out a loud growl, reminding him that he hasn't eaten since breakfast, and it was going on three o'clock.

He parked the rental car across the street from the building, which housed the CDC and cut off the engine. He would rather drive his large SUV, but here, it was important that he blended in. People were sure to remember a large black SUV driving around downtown.

This time the target was not considered to be hostile, but he was to be on the lookout just in case. They were unsure of just how much Dr. Amanda Bowers knew about the virus outbreak; it was up to him to make sure she didn't know anything.

From the dossier on Dr. Bowers, he discerned that she was thirty-three years old, unmarried, highly intelligent, and a workaholic. The one thing they did leave out, though, was that she was a very attractive woman.

She was the lead analyst at the Center for Disease Control and Prevention, and took her job very seriously. However, when he passed her on the street, he saw something that could indeed cause them a lot of trouble. There was compassion in her eyes. His gut told him that this particular woman would not see the benefits of what he was ordered to do. No, she was one of those who definitely stuck up for the underdog, which was bad for them.

Now, the man who worked under her could possibly be swayed to their way of thinking. Gary Wheeler's dossier read a lot differently than Dr. Bowers'. Yes, this was a man they would be able to manipulate anyway they wanted, especially if they threw money his way. He has an extreme amount of debt and could easily be bought.

The most interesting fact about Gary Wheeler was not his exorbitant amount of knowledge on flu pandemics, but that the CDC hired an outsider as his supervisor instead of promoting him.

***

Amanda Bowers was tired of waiting for the blood samples to come in. People were dying at an unbelievable rate, and she was determined to find out the cause. She tried to get her supervisors to understand exactly what she believed was happening here. It was no longer just about the numbers alone, but the underlying problems. It wouldn't be long before the public began to panic, and the medical staff was already reaching the point of being overwhelmed. The most frightening thing was just how fast the numbers were rising all across the United States.

The hospitals here in Atlanta have also had several cases of the virus walk through their doors; although, no deaths were reported as of yet. Perhaps, her being there in the forefront, she would be able to help prevent them.

She knocked on Dr. Bentley's door. "Sir, I hate to bother you again, but more deaths are being reported."

"What are we looking at with regards to the patient count so far?"

"Jane Foster is assimilating the actual number for you as we speak, but with each passing minute, the numbers are rising. The last good count we have is forty thousand."

Taking his glasses off, he cleaned the lenses, as he contemplated what she was telling him. "What about the patient profile?"

"At the current time, it is still mostly the elderly and high risk patients. The first to die were those with underlying illnesses such as heart disease, cancer patients, and HIV."

"Have you heard from the press yet?"

"No, sir, but I honestly feel this is just the tip of the iceberg."

"I don't believe it is time to step in just yet. I will authorize you to go and check out the local hospitals here to see just how they are handling this. As far as we can tell, everyone is doing their part."

"Sir, the one common denominator in all of these cases is inoculation with the flu vaccine within twenty four hours of onset of symptoms."

"You and I both know that is simply a coincidence. There are too many protocols in place for the vaccines to become contaminated."

***

Later that day, as soon as she walked into the Emergency Room at one of the local hospitals, she could see the chaos that has ensued here as well. At the receptionist's desk, she asked, "May I speak with the doctor on call?"

Without looking up, the nurse stated, "Dr. Young is on call tonight, but unfortunately, he is seeing a patient right now. If you would like, I can have him speak with you once he is available."

Without wasting a moment, she slipped her business card under the nurse's nose. "I believe he may want to make time to talk with me. Between the both of us, we may be able to treat these patients."

"Oh, I'm so sorry, Dr. Bowers; I thought perhaps you were a reporter wanting confirmation that the virus has reached Atlanta as well. They have been calling nonstop and we figured they would be visiting the hospital soon."

Over the PA, the nurse asked for Dr. Young to report to the receptionist's desk as soon as possible. A haggard young doctor made his way to the desk a few minutes after the announcement. "This better be good. I am trying to treat patients."

Without waiting for the nurse to introduce her, Amanda stepped forward. "Dr. Young, I apologize for the unannounced visit, but my name is Dr. Amanda Bowers with the CDC. I may be able to help you with regards to identifying this virus."

Dr. Young looked at her with genuine surprise. "Dr. Bowers, I didn't know that the CDC issued a bulletin about the virus."

She shook her head. "At this time, we have not. Several reports have come in from various states regarding deaths resulting from a virus strain. Unfortunately, their blood samples have not been received as of yet. I am hoping you will allow me the privilege to draw my own samples from the patients you are currently treating."

Dr. Young ran a hand through his hair. "I would more than welcome the opportunity." Dr. Young gestured his arm in front of her and said, "Right this way, Dr. Bowers."

"How are the patients?"

Looking around to make certain that no one was listening he answered, "Since this morning, we have seven more cases in this hospital. On a hunch, I called a few of the surrounding hospitals." He dropped his voice to almost a whisper, "All three of those hospitals have had an influx of patients as well."

"How many cases are we talking about?"

"There are thirty-two so far."

"Thirty-two cases of this strain of the flu have been admitted to the hospital in the last twelve hours? Why hasn't the CDC been notified?"

Dr. Young locked eyes with Dr. Bowers and stated emphatically. "To be honest with you, we have all been focusing more on saving lives rather than worrying about reporting the situation to the CDC. Some of the other doctors feel that this is nothing to be concerned with, and this is simply a sudden outbreak of the flu."

Dr. Bowers could feel the blood drain from her face. "You don't agree, do you?"

"No, I do not. Whatever this is, it hits the body fast and doesn't stop until the host is dead. Thankfully, it seems to die out fast with the host, without spreading to others."

"That is what we have been hearing from the other hospitals as well. There are some who do not believe that this is something for the CDC to be concerned with; however, I am not of that opinion. I believe that we are lucky so far that it has not mutated, but as with all viruses, there is a high probability that it will mutate and probably soon."

"I don't mind telling you, Dr. Bowers, that this particular virus scares the hell out of me. As a doctor, I do not like knowing that when a patient comes in there is nothing we can do to save his or her life. I am not content with simply sitting by and waiting for them to die. The sheer number of fatalities that we are likely to see could be staggering."

Amanda was busily organizing her own thoughts as she listened to him speak. "I completely agree, Dr. Young."

As they entered Exam Room 3, Dr. Young explained, "This is Bernice Holloway. She is eighty two years old and started feeling sick yesterday afternoon."

A shiver of fear snaked down Amanda's spine. The patient looked as if she has been sick for a lot longer than twenty four hours. She explained to Ms. Holloway, "I need to draw some blood. You will feel a tiny prick, but it is very important that I am able to get a blood sample."

The elderly lady barely had the strength to nod her head in understanding. After putting the tourniquet around the patient's arm, she swabbed the area over the large vein right in her elbow with rubbing alcohol. Amanda carefully inserted the butterfly needle attached to the blue-capped vacuum tube into her vein. She was clearly dehydrated, making it difficult to find the vein. For a moment, she thought the vein had rolled on her, but suddenly, a deep maroon colored venous blood spurted into the clear glass tube pulled by the vacuum. In a matter of only seconds, the tube was nearly full. To be on the safe side, Amanda filled three tubes before pressing a cotton swab against the area where the needle had penetrated the skin. She withdrew the needle quickly and held the swab for a few seconds to ensure the blood began to clot.

Applying a band aid over the cotton swab to hold it in place, Amanda smiled down at her, "Thank you. I hope you start to feel better soon."

Amanda shook the tubes gently to mix the blood with the anticoagulants already present in the tube. After carefully marking each tube with the patient's name and hospital number, she slipped them into the insulated cooler she brought with her. This testing would be done at her own facility.

Amanda continued on until she had obtained a sample from each patient in the hospital suffering from the flu. With each patient, she asked about their comings and goings during the days leading up to the illness, but very few of the patients could answer any of her questions. Since it was important that she obtain that information, she spoke to each member of the family at the hospital regarding the patient's activities during the days prior to the onset of the illness, in hopes of finding where each of them could have come into contact with the virus. As she stepped into the last room, she felt her blood run cold. Lying in the hospital bed was Henry, her security guard. As she had been trained to do so, she carefully put aside her personal feelings, and told him, "Henry, I am sorry to see that you are feeling worse. I must say, though, that I am quite impressed with this doctor here. You are in good hands."

Henry could barely find the strength to smile. "Uh-oh. Should I be worried that they have brought in the big guns for my case?"

She shook her head. "No, not at all. Dr. Young just called to let me know that there has been a sudden outbreak of the flu virus. You know how it is every year."

Her heart broke as she looked at the sweet, elderly man, though. His cheeks were gaunt with the shadow of approaching death. He looked far worse than when she last saw him. He seemed to have already become a skeleton. She watched as he struggled to breathe. His natural dark colored skin had a pastiness to it that she didn't like.

She listened as the rhythmic beeping of the EKG monitor changed with his erratic heartbeat. She quickly took the samples she needed and walked out of the room.

Once back in the hall, Amanda asked, "What about Gladys, his wife?"

Dr. Young looked at her with a grim expression. "His children and I have agreed not to tell him just yet since he is struggling to live, but she is at death's door. I don't give her much longer at all. I have a feeling they will be dying just hours, if not minutes apart. We had to move her, as her health is declining faster."

Amanda noticed that time seemed to fly by; she quickly performed her job of collecting samples to help her determine just what they were dealing with. Before leaving the hospital, she also obtained several urine samples, placing each sample she collected in sterilized bags and marking each carefully.

Before placing each sample in the ice chest containing dry ice, she double checked to make sure each sample was securely sealed. It was important not to have the carbon dioxide from the dry ice penetrate the samples. Once back at the CDC, she would instruct the lab on which tests she wanted run.

***

As Amanda left the hospital, she learned the sad news; Gladys succumbed to the virus. Henry was spared the news of her death. He drifted into a deep coma just minutes before her death. His children felt that he must have known the woman he loved with all his heart was dead and he gave up fighting the impossible. Exactly an hour after her passing away, Henry joined her in heaven.

Chapter 23

John Haskins looked at the sheer number of people standing in line at the clinic today and shuddered. Maybe a free flu shot wasn't worth this wait. He hadn't expected that there would be so many people at this hour. If he didn't watch it, he would be late for work. He has only been on Social Security Disability for about a year now, but when he was offered a part time job delivering newspapers, he jumped on the opportunity. It got him out of the house for a little bit, and it was the only job he could do.

Ever since the last back surgery, it has been hard to truly do much of anything. Throwing papers from a car was something he was capable of doing, though.

He watched the nurse administer the shots. After the fifth person received their shot, John realized that those who were here for the free shots were separated from the paying patients. Could it be that they were just trying to be nice to the disabled and elderly or was his paranoid mind running amuck? His wife was always accusing him of trying to find government conspiracies in even the littlest things.

John was surprised to find that this line was actually moving at a faster pace than the paying patients. Perhaps the free vaccine was simply a placebo? That didn't make sense, though; the government surely wouldn't want to spend more money than it needed to on health care. By giving them a placebo, they would be opening themselves up to even more medical expenses.

Perhaps, his wife was right and he did look for trouble where there was none. Maybe they were just being helpful here at the clinic was all. The longer they kept low immunity patients here, the easier it was for them to get sick. It would be better to get them in and out fast, rather than taking the chance of them catching something other than the flu.

As he got his shot, John found it surprising that the nurse kept all of her information in a small notebook. In this day and age, one would figure even the smaller clinics would use computers to keep track of who received a shot. He would never expect it to just be jotted down on a piece of paper.

By the time John made it home from his flu shot and delivering the newspapers, he could feel a fever starting. He could barely make it to his recliner before a stabbing pain in his stomach hit him. As the pain finally receded, he could feel his stomach actually gurgling.

He had no idea what was going on, but this was the worst he has felt in a very long time. Every time he got a flu shot, it seemed as if he actually did get the flu; except, this time it was worse. He had trouble breathing. It felt as if his chest was actually in a vise grip.

The nurse mentioned something about feeling bad for a bit after the shot, and maybe this was what she was referring to.

***

Dolores called out to her husband to come help her with the groceries. As she walked into the living room, she stopped in mid-sentence. Her husband has never looked worse than he did right now. His color was an ashen gray. When he stared up at her, it was like he was in a trance. His eyes were hollow, empty, and lifeless. He sounded more like he was wheezing, rather than breathing. He looked as if he aged twenty years over these last few hours. When she said goodbye to him this morning, he looked fine.

He croaked out, "I think I'm sick."

She leaned over and kissed his forehead. "You are burning up. How long have you been sick?"

"I just started feeling bad a few hours ago."

Delores grabbed her car keys and purse, "Come on. I need to get you to the emergency room."

****

Johnny Haskins, Jr. stared forward as if in a trance. These last few days have been a blur. Today, he was surrounded by family and friends, but he has never felt so alone in all of his twelve years.

Today, he felt as if he was in someone else's body. He was too shocked to believe that this was his life right now. His grandmother always told him that he has an old soul and today, he believed it may be true.

He heard the priest's words, but they held no real meaning to him. "Ashes to ashes, dust to dust..." There was a hum in the distance, as he continued to stare forward. This had to be a nightmare. His dad wasn't really dead.

He took in a deep breath. The air around him was heavy. He could smell the sweetness of the flowers, and the dampness of the earth began to fill his lungs. He tugged at the knot of the tie pinching his neck.

His life seemed impossible without his dad. His dad taught him so much. He loved him with all his heart and now he was gone. He was the person who taught him how to ride a bike. He was the one who instilled in him how to use his words and not his fists.

Tears filled his eyes once more. There would be no more late night heart to heart talks about girls and life in general. There would be no more pep talks early in the morning before school or a game.

As the priest's hand sliced through the misty air in the shape of a cross, an overwhelming sadness overcame Johnny. It was almost as if the priest was crossing his dad out of his life.

Johnny found his eyes drawn to the coffin that held his dad's body. This fancy box in no way resembled what his dad looked like; it was too pretentious, too decorative. His dad would have wanted something simpler.

His mom looked down at him and squeezed his hand. How Johnny wished his dad could be here to wrap his arms around him and hug him once more. That man inside the coffin did not even resemble his dad.

In the car on the way to the cemetery, he asked his mom once more if that man in the coffin was really his dad. From the loud sobs coming from her body, his greatest fears were confirmed.

As the coffin was lowered into the ground, he could feel the pitiful glances people made his way. His mother's looming presence brought him no comfort. As he threw a rose into the plot, his heart broke.

Four days ago, his dad had been fine and now he was dead. His death came quickly, from a simple flu strain. How could someone who has never truly been sick a day in his life, suddenly die from the flu? It didn't make sense to Johnny. His dad had gone in and gotten the flu shot just like he had been told to. That shot was supposed to keep you from getting sick, but instead, he watched his dad being laid to rest.

Chapter 24

Jeffery Wilkinson shuffled about his house, leaning heavily on his cane. The thick carpet made it harder for him to walk. The fibers caught on the soles of his shoes and tugged at the rubber tip of the cane. He may have to take his daughter's advice and remove the carpet his late wife loved so much. It was no longer the pretty beige that it had once been. The dirt trapped in it made it look more like a light brown.

As he moved into the living room, he could feel his age catching up with him. At one time, he was well over six feet tall, but now, he could not look anyone in the eye; instead, his gaze greeted them at chest level. His once muscular body was all bent and twisted from the ravages of time. He could feel his age in his joints and muscles, and today, it hurt to move or even blink.

He probably should call his daughter to come help him, but he didn't want to burden her more than he needed to. He felt so useless, a waste of space on this earth; besides, he could manage without anyone's help. He has done well all alone these last five years after his wife's death.

After he finally made it to the living room, he dropped into his favorite recliner, propped up his feet, and turned on the television. He regretted letting his daughter take him to the doctor to get a flu shot. He had no plans to get the blasted thing, but Barbara heard this flu season was supposed to be the worst one ever and she feared that one of her kids would bring it home from school.

Besides, the shot was free for him this year just like she said. This may be the first thing the government has ever done that didn't cost him a dime.

He despised going to the clinic, though, and almost insisted on going to his regular doctor. Jeffery always prided himself on how hard he worked to make a living. He was not like most of the whining welfare grabbing kids that had been there at the clinic today; all of them waiting for their free handouts. No, he had never once been like that. He came from a time when people took responsibility for themselves and where they took care of themselves. Hell, he made it through the Great Depression and through the wars just fine, because he was a survivor.

Time may age his body, but it could not change who or what he was.

As he closed his eyes for a nap, he was transported back in time onto the US Navy ship during Pearl Harbor. He could feel the danger in the air; it was as if the atmosphere around all of them was charged.   Yes, if he could survive Pearl Harbor, then he could survive a measly flu shot. He just needed to sleep a bit he told himself.

***

The body of Jeffrey Wilkinson was outlined by a sheet. By the side of his bed was his daughter, Rebecca, along with her husband, Graham. Graham consoled his wife, as she stared at the outline of what had once been her loving father.

In a soft voice, almost as if she was afraid to wake the deceased, "I don't understand it. I just saw him yesterday morning and he was fine. There was nothing wrong with him."

The doctor wished he could bring her some comfort. "The illness moved through his body very fast." As he reviewed the notes he had on his clipboard, he asked, "Were you aware that your father had Stage 4 lung cancer?"

She let out a startled gasp, "What, no he never even mentioned it."

Nodding, he continued, "It could be that he may not have known, as well, but it helped the virus to progress as fast as it did. His body was already trying to fight off the cancer, and when the influenza invaded his body, it just didn't know which one to fight off. His immune system was already severely compromised."

With tears in her eyes, she replied, "I guess we should be grateful that he died as fast as he did. It is heartbreaking that he died all alone. If only I could have been there for him."

Chapter 25

Dr. Amanda Bowers tried to focus on the words in front of her, but they were a blur. She rubbed her tired eyes.

She has been at this for hours now, but it felt like days. At three o'clock this morning, she had awakened and no matter how hard she tried, she just couldn't go back to sleep. The answer to what was going on had to be staring her right in the face, but she just couldn't seem to find it.

She made herself a pot of coffee and got dressed. She knew she was forfeiting a good night's sleep. By four a.m., she was at her desk researching viral outbreaks.

She poured over long research studies and resources, hoping to find anything similar to what they were dealing with, but so far, she has had no luck.

She let out a long yawn, before heading to the coffee pot. After pouring herself another cup, she searched other parts of the world for evidence verifying they have had the same virus there as well. It was not uncommon for other areas to have outbreaks of a fatal illness.

She found plenty of photos of people covered in white sheets, lining makeshift hospital rooms in huge tents, but she found nothing similar to what she was searching for.

She feared that if they didn't do something soon, they would be facing a worse epidemic than in 1918, where the influenza outbreak killed between twenty and forty million people. Unfortunately, that was throughout the globe, and this virus was limited to the United States.

Just as she was about ready to stretch, she received a notification from another hospital. The doctor there not only sent a request, but a picture of what they were dealing with. She shivered at the sight in front of her. These people were lying in hospital beds just waiting to die.

The patients' eyes staring back at her were vacant, hollow, and completely devoid of life. Right now, the complete medical field here in the United States seemed to be powerless, as they fought a force far stronger than modern medicine.

Currently, they couldn't even develop a vaccine to help prevent this virus, because they had no idea what they were fighting. Hell, they couldn't even figure out just how the disease spread. The only thing that the patients had in common was that they all took the vaccine before coming down with the flu.

At first, Amanda contemplated that there could be a bad batch of vaccine, but not everyone receiving the vaccine has come down with the flu. They were still in the process of tracking down the batch number being used, but so far, all the clinics were reporting back with the same answer--a government employee through Medicare came in and inoculated the patients.

Medicare reported that they have no information with regards to the inoculation. They were still unclear as to how the letter with regards to the free vaccines went out; no one wanted to admit knowledge of this as well. Talk about one hand not knowing what the other was doing.

Chapter 26

Kevin Jameson looked at the map on the computer screen in front of him. The display was a detailed composite of satellite imagery for the entire United States. All he had to do was click on a particular area and it became clearer.

He took his time clicking on each area and watched as the map zoomed in. Visible on the map were red dots indicating areas given the vaccines, white dots indicated areas still waiting for the vaccines and black dots indicated areas reporting deaths. This map was the only computerized documentation of the vaccinations.

He would have to wait until later this afternoon to find out any further information. Miranda would overnight her notes on who received the shot and who was now deceased.

From another screen, he pulled up the CDC's National Environmental Health Tracking Network. It had been too easy to hack into this. From here, he was also able to track down what the CDC suspected as well.

As soon as a doctor, hospital, or clinic feared that a patient in their office or facility had the newest strain of the flu, they alerted the CDC, who updated their files immediately. This helped them make sure that the flu had not spread. So far, the flu has stayed confined to those who received the vaccine. The number of deaths right away was staggering. Most of the elderly patients being inoculated died within forty eight hours of the injection. This was faster than the prisoners.

Kevin looked away from the computer screen and stared at the ceiling. His office was nothing more than a windowless cubicle. Standing up and stretching, he stepped outside of his office.

He had been inside longer than he would have liked. The harsh sunlight caused him to blink several times before his eyes adjusted.

So much that deals with this particular project was unclear to him. The orders he was given bear no resemblance to what these government officials were supposed to uphold in the Constitution.

It took everything inside of him to proceed. He wondered if the same could be said for the man who issued the order. Could he sleep at night knowing he ordered the deaths of all these unsuspecting citizens?

Kevin knew that the research has been done, but did they truly understand this virus? Were they certain that it could not be transferred to others?

From all the research he has done on his own, he knew that rhinoviruses and flu were very clever. They were profligate and mutated rapidly in order to survive.

If that was the case, it wouldn't be long before this virus injected into these chosen hosts began to mutate and spread. Flu viruses were smarter than those doing the research. They were evolving constantly and through the years found ways to transfer from host to host.

It tore him up on the inside that Americans were dying, and he was part of the group that helped to do this. His own government was willing to sacrifice millions of Americans in order to save money.

He tried to tell himself that death was part of the human life cycle, but a part of him reminded him that what they were doing was wrong. Families were left grieving because a loved one has died unexpectedly. They were left in shock, and he was partially to blame for bringing grief to them.

That simple fact was almost too much to bear. No matter how they tried to justify these deaths, they were still nothing more than death at the hand of an assassin. These were murders; pure and simple. This was a homicide for political and social justifications.

So far, no one outside his chain of command, or his direct chain of command to the White House, has any idea what was going on. How long would it be before someone began to suspect and started to question? The CDC would eventually obtain a sample of patient blood and they would run tests. There was no way they could prevent that.

If the media caught wind of what could possibly be happening, it wouldn't be long before conspiracy theories were thrown around; those very theories wouldn't be far from the truth.

Chapter 27

Dr. Johnson groaned as he turned up the windshield wipers in his car. When would this rain ever stop?

He slowed down for a curve on the slick road. Christmas was only a few weeks away and this year he was literally in no holiday mood.

As he hit a pothole, the impact bounced his car so hard he thought for sure he would get a flat tire. The coffee he was holding splashed up out of the lid and down the side of to cup from the harsh impact.

As a Christmas song came on the radio, "Peace on earth, goodwill towards men…" he shut off the radio. There was no amount of music that could help lift his spirits today.

Suddenly, his safe, sane world has taken a strange turn. Patients were dying and there was nothing he could do about it. His standing orders were as soon as a flu patient came in, they were to have labs drawn. Those with labs that came back confirming the newest strain of the virus were to be taken up to the fifth floor and isolated from the other patients. Even though the virus has not spread, he refused to take any chances.

There were only a handful of nurses and doctors that handled these cases. The CDC felt that he was being overly cautious, but he didn't think so.

He worried that the deaths were putting a strain on the staff at the hospital as well. The cheerful staff seemed to have the same mood as he did. Day after day, they cared for patients with the incurable virus. It moved quicker than any other strain they have ever dealt with. At least it killed the patient quickly.

What especially bothered him, besides the sheer number of deaths, was all the deaths seemed to occur not long after their vaccination. So far, the only thing these patients did have in common was the inoculation. It was ludicrous to even consider that there could be something wrong with the vaccine.

He rubbed his eyes, as the fatigue and stress of the week caught up with him. His cell phone beeped, alerting him to his low battery. He was so busy today that he never had a chance to put it on the charger. He tossed it on the passenger seat instead of bothering with charging it. He wasn't too far from the house anyway.

Rubbing his eyes once more, he wished the coffee he had earlier would at least kick in for a few minutes. He corrected his steering once more, as the lines of the road morphed together and then apart, similar to a dance.

As he rounded a sharp corner of the road, headlights shined in his rear view mirror. He shook his head at just how insane the driver of the other vehicle was acting. The car was closing in fast and with these wet roads, it was just an accident waiting to happen.

Easing up on the gas, he moved as far off the road as he could to allow the vehicle to pass him, but instead of passing him, it stayed on his tail. Its front bumper was almost touching his back bumper.

He slowed down a little more, hoping the car would finally pass him. It wasn't until he drove at a snail's pace that the dark car finally passed him.

Just as he was gathering speed, he saw a pair of headlights coming right for him. He swerved just in time to miss having a head on collision; however, with the wet road surface, his vehicle began to spin out of control.

Forcing his mind to stay calm, he managed to right the vehicle before it hit a tree. His heart pounded against his chest wall, as he gasped for air. It has been a long time since he was in an accident, even if this was simply a near miss.

As he gathered his thoughts, it suddenly dawned on him that this was no accident. The car that passed him earlier was the same one that just tried to hit him head on. Which meant that the same vehicle would more than likely come back to ensure the job had been successful.

As he made his way back on the road, he kept his headlights turned off. While pulling out, he noticed a vehicle making a slow approach to where he just went off the road. He couldn't make it out, but he was fairly certain that it was the same one that just tried to kill him.

He had no doubt in his mind that whoever was driving wanted him dead, but who would want him dead? He had no enemies that he knew of. He was just a simple doctor working in the emergency room of a run of the mill hospital.

Then the reality hit him like a ton of bricks. He has been asking a lot of questions and talking to the CDC about his suspicions with regards to a deadly flu virus.

As soon as the thought entered his mind, he began to scold himself; there was no conspiracy here. Besides, he has worked with the CDC before, and they always alerted the public. They were even working together with this current epidemic.

Yeah, and it just so happened that not only was the CDC not receiving the blood samples collected for them, but a dark car was now trying to run you off the road. He has never been one to buy into all the conspiracy theories, but he had to admit right now those same people he considered nut jobs may have been on to something.

Chapter 28

Amanda barely made it to the office when her secretary stopped her, "You may as well not get too comfortable." She handed Amanda a plane ticket and itinerary. "You are needed at a hospital in Michigan. They called in with the same reports as down here. The CDC needs you there to see if this is anything to be concerned with."

"What are my orders?"

"You are to assess the situation, send samples, and report back here. If it appears that we may indeed have an epidemic, we will have to rethink the situation."

Amanda looked down at the itinerary and saw that her plane left in an hour. That gave her very little time to get there. Hell, as big as the Atlanta airport was, it could take up to half an hour from checking in to get to your gate. Thankfully, she was a firm believer in always being prepared. She kept a go bag packed at all times; one here in the office and one in the trunk of her car. That way if she ever needed to, she could just drop everything and go.

As the plane took off, Amanda finally let her mind absorb what she was about to do. She feared that more cases would pop up, and it appeared that she had been right. However, she hoped it would be contained to the southern states. There was quite a bit of distance between here and Michigan. She needed to ascertain if any of the patients traveled to the affected states or if a member of their family has recently been there. There had to be a connection.

She had an idea of what to expect and what was expected of her this time. This time she knew what to look for. The fear that this virus has become communicable also weighed heavy on her mind.

As with her trip to Louisiana, Amanda didn't bother to check into her hotel first. She had the taxi cab drive her straight to the hospital. The hospital here in Michigan was the polar opposite of the hospital in Springport. This hospital was constructed in a modern style and three times the size of the other hospital.

The entrance was floored with a highly polished travertine that echoed the sound of shoes hitting the tile. A young, perky receptionist directed her to the administrative offices located on the third floor. She was greeted there by another young receptionist, and Amanda wondered if there was a pattern to the hiring here. "Dr. Bowers, Mr. Frank Levine is waiting for you in the conference room." She stood up and escorted Amanda to the room. Before opening the door, she asked, "Can I get you something to drink?"

"A cup of coffee would be nice."

Without warning, the door opened and Amanda found herself having to take a step backward, as a man relieved her of her suitcase. "I thought I heard voices out here." The man stated, as he enthusiastically shook her now free hand, "I am Frank Levine the hospital administrator. We have been patiently waiting for you."

The man in front of her was like no hospital administrator she has ever met; instead, he looked as if he could have walked right out of a current GQ men's magazine. He was well over six feet tall with broad shoulders. His green eyes drew you in and were a striking contrast to his wavy dark brown hair.

"We are very grateful that you could come so quickly."

"I am sure that by now you are well aware of what is happening in Louisiana and a few other states. I am here to see if we are indeed dealing with the same problem here."

"Yes, yes of course. Since calling the CDC, fourteen more cases have been admitted. Of the thirty three cases admitted for treatment, twenty have passed away already and four are in critical condition."

Amanda sank into the chair, as she listened to the overwhelming news. "Can you tell me what else you have learned so far?"

Shaking his head, he replied, "I am afraid not much. I had hoped that the doctors working on these cases could meet with you as well, but they are extremely busy at this time."

"There will be time for me to talk to them. I understand that their first priority is to the patients."

"The first case was admitted yesterday morning. At first, we were not alarmed. It wasn't until the numbers grew to twenty five cases and none of the patients were showing any sign of improvement that Dr. Talbot decided to sound the alarm and call you."

Amanda asked, "Has any lab work been done?"

"A full work up has been done on all the patients."

Amanda nodded her head, "I would prefer to review those reports before I see the patients or talk to the doctors."

"Yes, yes of course. I totally understand."

Handing her a stack of patient charts, he explained, "I already had a copy made of what we have so far on the patients."

As Amanda started to glance over the records, she asked, "Have you been able to make any association with at least one of the patients and an affected state?"

Mr. Levine shook his head, "No, we asked each of the patients if they traveled recently or knew someone that did so. So far, we have made no connection. Most of the patients don't even know anyone down there."

Amanda tapped her pen on the table, "Hmmm, there is always the chance that they just had a brief contact with someone visiting. I need to start making a detailed timeline to find a connection."

Mr. Levine contemplated all that she was saying. "That will be like searching for a needle in a haystack, won't it?"

Amanda nodded her head in agreement, "Yes, it will." She began stacking the folders and said, "Perhaps, I should see the patients."

In the elevator, Mr. Levine informed Amanda, "When the patient numbers started increasing, we decided it would be better to change things up a bit. The maternity ward has been moved to one of our private room floors. Then, we turned the maternity ward into the isolation ward. The isolation ward that we had earlier is no longer big enough to handle the patient numbers coming in. Once the previous isolation ward is decontaminated, we can decide if it should be used as the maternity ward for now."

"In my honest opinion, I wouldn't use it for a maternity ward at this time, not until we know exactly what we are dealing with."

As Amanda obtained samples from the patients, she could see that each patient's conditions were deteriorating fast. She doubted most of these patients would survive the day, much less see tomorrow.

From what Amanda has seen of the lab work and the patients, this was the same virus that was killing patients elsewhere.

 "Did you happen to find out if any of the patients received a flu shot before the onset of symptoms?"

Mr. Levine shook his head. "I don't believe that is a question any of the doctors even considered. Why? Did that make a difference?"

"I am just curious is all."

After she collected all the samples and packaged them for shipment to the CDC, she called her supervisor, Dr. Bentley. Her phone conversation was short and to the point. "We are dealing with the same strain of influenza."

"Were you able to ascertain if anyone infected was in contact with anyone from an affected state?"

Amanda paused as she talked to him. "Here is the thing. All of my initial tests confirm that this is not a communicable disease, and we all know that influenza is. I have sent the samples to be tested, but at this time, I believe that we have separate incidents."

"You may as well come back to Atlanta for now. Make sure they set up the same protocols as elsewhere."

"Yes, sir, but do you mind if I ask a few more questions? I am anxious to find out just how the influenza is spreading."

"Just be back to Atlanta this afternoon. I have a feeling we may be called to another city before long."

Amanda feared the same thing, which was why she had certain questions she wanted to ask.

***

With a heavy heart, she told Mr. Levine that she would be heading back to Atlanta. She explained that she would be more beneficial to them back in her office to run the needed tests. As Amanda flew back, she went over all that she acquired about this outbreak.

She did want to do some more research, though. Every one of the patients she talked to did indeed receive a flu vaccine recently. She plans on finding out just how many patients in the affected states received the flu vaccine. She also needed to get her hands on a sample of the vaccine from one of the clinics handing them out, it must be tested for contamination.

She hated making a diagnosis when there was no available treatment. The fact that she discovered the only connection between the affected sites was the vaccine could not be merely a coincidence.

Chapter 29

Before hanging up the phone, Miranda Hamilton said a simple phrase, "It is done." She stared at the phone, as it went in and out of focus from the tears welling up in her eyes.

It's funny how her life changed so much over these last few months. Honestly, she never thought she was capable of what she has done, nor would she have believed that the government was capable of ordering the deaths of so many innocent people.

She wasn't capable of visualizing the deaths and the horror that she would be causing. Her phone beeped, acknowledging that she had a text message. "You leave at three a.m. for your next destination. It is imperative that this mission be completed."

***

Kevin Jameson picked up the phone. "I believe Miranda may be a problem."

"The results are pleasing. Maybe it is time to move into the next phase a little earlier than anticipated. Can you handle Miranda?"

"It will all be taken care of, sir."

"I don't have to remind you what is riding on the confidentiality of this project."

Kevin replied, "No, sir; you don't."

After hanging up, he made another call. "It is time to begin the next phase. Are you ready?"

"Yes, sir. The shipments are ready to go. They will be at each of the health clinics first thing in the morning."

Kevin informed him, "Good. It is imperative that each clinic receives the strict orders that go with each delivery."

"Understood, sir."

Now that all his other orders were taken care of, it was time for him to take care of Miranda. He could tell that she was close to breaking. After that, he would begin to systematically remove the others from the equation as well. Once he was done, there would be no one left to talk.

Chapter 30

Jessica Lathrup held her breath as she looked around the office once more. She tried to act as normal as possible before walking into her supervisor's office. If the security guard caught her on the camera, she needed to make it look as if she truly was supposed to be there.

She considered coming into work early one morning, but that would raise eyebrows. She has no business being at work in the wee hours of the morning, but if she got caught right now, it could be explained as simply forgetting to put something on Miranda's desk.

Her plan seemed so easy in her mind. All she had to do was get in, get what she needed, and get out. It couldn't be any easier, but the one exception to that thought was nothing was ever as easy as it seemed here. There was an almost impregnable security system here designed to prevent precisely what she was about to do.

Right now, she wished like hell she had not overheard the conversation between Randy Erickson and Miranda. It truly was none of her business that Miranda had suddenly developed a conscience and was upset with this project she was working on. Jessica had not been briefed on the project, which meant it should be no business of hers in the first place. She should just do her own job and not worry about what has upset Miranda, but now that she knew about the details of the project, it bothered her that the government would do such a thing.

This was her only chance. The security protocols were disabled for only a brief moment. As soon as she was in Miranda's office, it took a moment for her eyes to focus. Jessica had no intention of turning the lights on in here. Thankfully, Miranda's office had no windows, which meant the office was bathed in darkness, not even her computer monitor was on.

As Jessica gently opened the desk drawer, she was thankful that Miranda had such an extreme case of obsessive compulsive disorder. There, in her secret hiding spot, was the Biohazard sign that has become a familiar sight here in the office these last several months.

She just stared at the small vial for a moment. It amazed her that something so small and light could be so deadly. Just a small drop of this would cause severe illness and eventually death. A vision of dying children and elderly people ran through her mind. Repulsion for what they were doing flowed through her body.

She advised her dad not to take the flu vaccine this year, without giving him a specific reason. Jessica slipped one of the small containers in her purse and headed out.

With each step towards the exit, anxiety built up inside of her. She still couldn't believe that she was doing this. She swore that she could feel the small vial bump up against her hip, even though it was not possible. The vaccine vial was safely secured in a container inside of her purse.

The hard part was over. She had managed to get inside Miranda's office without detection. She was almost outside of the office building, and she would find someone who could help her get the story out to the public.

Her hands were now shaking uncontrollably. She took a slow breath to calm her nerves, as she started her car.

Tears began to fill her eyes as the engine refused to start. She blinked back hot, frustrated tears. This couldn't be happening to her, not now.

She looked around the deserted parking lot to see if anyone was around. She purposefully stayed a few minutes late and now, there was no one here to help her. She reminded herself that was the plan after all. She had to linger later than the others, so she could gather the final evidence she needed. It hasn't been easy, but she finally managed to get it.

Now, what was she to do? She was stuck here in the dark with a car that wouldn't start. She let her head drop down, as she felt depression move into her body. She felt so deflated and helpless.

A sharp rap on the driver's side window caused her to jump. Randy Erickson, her supervisor, was outside trying to get her attention.

She opened the door, surprised to see him still here. "Is everything okay?"

He was the last person she wanted to see tonight. It was as if this man had an uncanny sense of knowing when something was wrong. As she went to speak, she prayed her voice didn't quiver. If he knew what she had in her bag, she was doomed, "My car won't start."

"Pop the hood. Do you happen to know how old the battery is?"

Jessica shrugged her shoulders, "I believe it is about three years old, but I'm not so sure."

Randy informed her, "It is probably your battery then. Try and start the car again, so I can see what happens."

Jessica turned the key in the ignition once more, but she only heard the sound of a click. "It sounds like the battery. Do you happen to have jumper cables?"

"Yeah, I should. I think there is an emergency kit in the trunk."

"Well, let's see if there is so I can give you a jump."

As she popped open her trunk, she glanced over at her purse. For a moment, a pang of regret filled her for what she planned on doing, but she then remembered what was at stake. *No, she was doing the right thing.*

As if sensing she was nervous, he tried to ease her distress, "Don't worry. I am sure that we can get your car started. If not, I will bring you home."

As Randy walked to his car, Jessica said a quick prayer that the car would start. The last thing she needed was Randy driving her home, especially since she had no plans of going home.

She watched as he pulled his car right in front of hers. He raised the hood of his car and attached the cables. She crossed her fingers, hoping that this works. Once his car was started, he signaled for her to do the same. A smile formed across her face, as her engine roared to life.

As he removed the cables, she walked over to him, "Thank you so very much."

Dusting off his hands after closing both hoods he replied, "No problem. I would go out and get a new battery as soon as possible, though. There is a chance that the battery won't start again and someone may not be around to jump you off again."

"I was just thinking the exact same thing." She smiled over at him, "Have a good night, Randy."

When she got back in her car, she let out a deep sigh. As she left the parking lot, she gave him a short beep and waved on her way out. Since he knew her normal route home, she would have to leave that same way and double back to where she was actually headed.

What she didn't know was that Randy killed the engine to his car, locked the doors, and headed back into the office, instead of leaving.

Jessica made a left out of the parking lot, turned right at the next two intersections, before entering the ramp onto the interstate. Once on the interstate, she let out a deep breath. She needed to stop and think about what she was going to do. If she wanted to survive this, there was no way she could do it half-cocked.

For tonight, she decided it would be better for her to head home. With Miranda out of the office, there would be no one there to notice that the vial was even missing. She could keep her ear to the ground and at the first mention that they believed something was missing, she could disappear. There was no reason to cause alarm just yet, especially since she was unsure of what to do with this information.

She turned on the radio and let the soft music soothe her frazzled nerves. She let out a deep breath, unaware that she had even been holding it.

Suddenly, she felt claustrophobic in the tiny car. She cracked open her window slightly, letting in some fresh air. The moonlight was so bright tonight there was no need for high beams.

The vacant road allowed her the opportunity to let her mind wander over all that she learned these last few days. Her brain whirled, as she played back the events; her body was on autopilot driving her straight home.

***

Randy walked around the offices once more to see if there was anything missing. It was not like Jessica Lathrup to work late. He saw from the security cameras that she entered Miranda's office, but as far as he could tell, she didn't take anything. Hell, he couldn't even figure out why the woman went in there. She didn't even turn on the lights. If she was looking for something, she must have known exactly where it was. From what he could tell, though, nothing in Miranda's office had been moved. Miranda's computer terminal hasn't even been turned on since her departure. Damn, he wished like hell he knew why she stayed late. He hated making this call, "I hate to bother you, but we may have a problem. Jessica Lathrop stayed late tonight. She came into Miranda's office, but I can't see where she tampered with anything."

Kevin Jameson muttered a curse under his breath, "Do you have any idea what she was after?"

"No, Miranda's computer wasn't turned on nor was the lights. She wasn't in there long either, in and out."

"Well, watch her closely. I will put a GPS tracker on her car so that we can keep track of her movements. I will also have someone watch her house starting tonight, just in case she plans on skipping town."

Randy honestly couldn't see Jessica doing anything wrong. She was a surprisingly shy girl, had difficulty at times looking someone in the eye when being introduced and above all else, she avoided confrontation.

Chapter 31

Dr. Johnson listened to the phone message once more and tried to decide if he should return the reporter's telephone call. The public had a right to know what they could be dealing with, but at this time, they don't even know what they were dealing with. However, he felt that he was on the brink of discovering something, and there was someone out there who was afraid of the same thing.

He was positive the accident the other day was no accident. Someone had tried to run him off the road. That night he was too scared to even go home. He waited two days before going back to his house, only to find that someone had tossed everything inside. He didn't even bother calling the police or checking his computer. If this was some kind of conspiracy, there was a chance that whoever was responsible more than likely bugged his phone, computer, and even his house.

Speaking to this reporter, Christopher Allen, may be the only way to find out the truth, as to what they were dealing with. The CDC was trying to be helpful, but he suspected even their hands were tied.

He has talked to Dr. Bowers on several occasions, each time promising to help get results, but so far, she hasn't been able to obtain definite results either.

Picking up his phone, he called Christopher Allen. "Mr. Allen, this is Dr. Johnson over at St. Anne General Hospital.

You left me a message earlier, and I am just now able to return my calls."

"Thank you for calling me back, Dr. Johnson. If you have a few minutes, there are some questions I would like to ask you."

"I can answer some of your basic questions, but to be honest with you, I don't have all the answers." Sighing, he added, "I must warn you, though, that I don't think this is something we should talk about over the phone. Is there a place we can meet in person?"

Chris asked, "Did you want to meet at my office?"

"No, I think it would be better for the both of us if no one knew we were meeting just now."

"I know a little out of the way restaurant where we can meet and no one will bother us."

"Are you busy now?" Dr. Johnson asked.

***

After making the arrangements, Chris hurried out of his office. He could feel the excitement building inside of him. It has been a long time since he covered a story like this.

When he arrived at the restaurant, he saw Dr. Johnson already seated at a back table or who he presumed was Dr. Johnson by the haggard look on his face. Christopher walked up to the man, "Dr. Johnson?"

Dr. Johnson extended his hand, "Mr. Allen."

After making himself comfortable at the table, he started, "Thank you for making time for me, Dr. Johnson." Taking out a notebook and tapping his pen on the paper he asked, "I'm not sure where to start, to be honest with you. How many people do you believe have been infected now?"

Running a hand down his drawn, grim face Dr. Johnson replied, "We are at two hundred confirmed deaths and there are another one hundred seventy five admitted in the hospital right now. The survival rate at this time is zero percent."

Christopher could hardly believe his ears. "Do you know if the other hospitals are reporting the same numbers?"

"Unfortunately, yes. The only good thing we have going for us right now is not everyone who came in with the flu symptoms have this particular strain of virus. There have been a number of patients coming in at the first sign of a runny nose, just because they are scared they have contracted the virus as well. It keeps us busy, but I would rather they come in and get tested, rather than take a chance. We are hoping that a patient will come in who does indeed have the virus and we can save them. It may be that early detection is the key."

"Does the general public need to be more concerned?"

Dr. Johnson shrugged his shoulders. "At this time, we still do not know a lot about this particular virus. We are not sure if the ones who have not contracted the virus are simply immune to it or what exactly keeps them from contracting it. It won't be too long before we do see people walking around with surgical masks and gloves. I can't guarantee that will do them any good, though."

Christopher nodded his head in agreement. "I do know from experience that people will buy just about anything when the decision is based on survival." Chris tapped his pen on the paper, as he contemplated his next question, "How long before the hospital is at its full capacity?"

"There have been some meetings to discuss which places can be used if this does indeed turn out to be an epidemic. Unfortunately, the fatality rate is so fast at this time that we do not have to worry about lack of space."

"Do you believe that if it comes down to it, they will start erecting tents?"

Dr. Johnson replied, "To be honest with you, I am not sure what the protocol will be until we know more about what we are fighting."

"What about the federal government? Have they stepped in to offer help as of yet?"

"The CDC is involved, of course, but at this time, no actual federal help has been offered."

Chris sat back in his chair and contemplated the lack of federal government help. "Don't you find that odd? It seems that as soon as a hurricane hits, FEMA is on our doorstep, offering as much help as they can."

"With more and more becoming infected every day, I have a feeling it won't be long now before the federal government does step in. The CDC is looking at a vaccine, but there are so many steps involved in that process and at the rate this virus is killing people, the vaccine may be too late."

Chris looked Dr. Johnson directly in the eyes, "I have noticed a trend in those dying. It seems as if the infected are mostly elderly or those with a weakened immune system already."

Dr. Johnson looked over at this reporter, wondering just how much he could trust him. "As a doctor, I have noticed the same thing." Leaning in, he whispered, "I have also noticed that every one of my patients affected by this virus was just inoculated with the flu vaccine."

That very statement floored Chris. "Have you asked anyone else if they noticed the same thing?"

"Let's just say that there are a few of us curious as to how these particular individuals are all contracting the virus."

Chris sat in silence, as his mind tried to absorb the information Dr. Johnson just gave him. "Surely, it just has to be a coincidence."

"All I know is Medicare and Medicaid ordered cutbacks on what they would pay for covered costs and all of a sudden, they are authorizing free inoculations to those using them. Those same patients are now dying at an alarming rate. I have never been one for conspiracy theories, but suddenly, I find myself reconsidering a lot of what I have believed."

"But, I just can't see the government approving the deaths of all these people. That is more like something Adolph Hitler would have done."

Dr. Johnson looked around the room before stating. "Just stop and think about how political officials have been warning us that social security benefits will be exhausted before long. Now, stop and think about the trillions the government owes. One way to alleviate some of the debt is to lessen the number of people draining that very system."

Chris could hardly believe his ears. "Do you have any evidence to prove that the virus came from the vaccine?"

"No, I don't, but the CDC has tried to obtain a sample of the vaccine, and as far as I know, they have had no luck."

Now, this was getting curious. Dr. Johnson informed him, "We have talked to several of the patients' families and none of those catching the virus have traveled anywhere, other than to get the vaccine. The only common denominator is in fact the vaccine, as far as I can tell."

As the restaurant started to get crowded, Chris could tell Dr. Johnson was getting nervous, "Why don't we talk again in a few days? I am sure you want to get home and rest."

Dr. Johnson stood up. "I don't believe I have had a good night's sleep since this all started. I should warn you to be extremely careful. The other night on my way home, someone actually ran me off the road."

"Do you think that it has something to do with the virus?"

"I am starting to think that."

***

Christopher Allen just looked at the computer screen in front of him. This was all just too unbelievable; the numbers in front of him were surely wrong. The death rate has increased dramatically in the last twenty four hours.

As he was about to turn off the television, the local news caught his attention. A female journalist was standing in front of St. Anne General Hospital. "The infection rate here in Springport, Louisiana has spread dramatically in the last forty eight hours. Bill Gaudet confirmed that they would be admitting anyone infected with the disease from surrounding hospitals. In turn, they will be sending the medical emergencies they normally receive to the other hospitals. This is a precaution in hopes of keeping the infected in a general location, without having to worry about infecting those who have minor emergencies. A triage has been set up here and other hospitals for anyone wanting to confirm if they do have the virus. Symptoms include extremely high fever, a severe cough, and dehydration.

"Most of the patients being admitted have all complained that it felt like a bad case of the flu, unfortunately this one could be fatal. The members of the medical community are begging anyone who feels the slightest bit sick to please come in and get checked out. The hospitals, in hopes of encouraging people to come in to be checked, are offering this service free of charge."

Looking directly into the camera now, the reporter continued, "We have learned that Springport is not the only community dealing with this deadly virus. Several other cities have also confirmed that they are indeed fighting this same virus; unfortunately, they are all experiencing the same outcomes. Stay tuned for more details as they become available."

Damn, Chris thought to himself. He had hoped to have this as a front page story in the morning before the news was broadcast all over, but it looked as if they were on top of things as well. All he could do right now was hope that they haven't discovered that the patients all have the same thing in common, the vaccine.

Chapter 32

Dr. Johnson walked into the locker room and changed into his scrubs. As he prepared to begin his shift, the PA system came to life. For a short period of time, the area was quiet as everyone waited for the announcement. This was one of the only times the hospital was ever clothed in a heavy stillness, as everyone waited for the news of what was to come. "Priority One involving a motor vehicle accident times two. Three victims, one critical. Pregnant woman with life threatening injuries."

When he walked into the Emergency Room, it was already full with patients and now, a motor vehicle accident was added to these waiting patients.

Once the notice came through, everyone moved into action quickly; all around him was a frenzy of activity. Nurses were busy preparing the trauma rooms and making sure the equipment was ready. X-ray technicians wheeled out portable machines as lab technicians prepare to draw blood. An orthopedic surgeon as well as an Ob/Gyn doctor rushed into the ER.

Interns lined up ready for orders to be barked at them. Dr. Johnson was happy to have interns working here with him. He has never seen a more confident group than those working here.

The patients in the waiting room sensed that something was happening. They looked around and watched the activity around them, as if they wondered what could have happened. Without warning, the doors burst open and gurneys flooded in.

The pregnant woman was wheeled in first. She was pale, which meant that she had lost a lot of blood. The Ob/Gyn moved away a strand of hair from her face and asked, "Can you hear me?"

Instead of answering, she moaned softly in pain. The paramedic informed him, "The baby's heart rate is dropping. There was no way we could make it to another hospital."

The OB doctor barked out orders, "Let's get an ultrasound ASAP. I want to know what we are dealing with before we do an emergency C-section."

Dr. Johnson moved on to another patient when the paramedic quickly told him, "From what we can tell, this man was the one who caused the accident. He wasn't wearing a seat belt and was thrown from the vehicle."

Dr. Johnson looked down at his patient and suspected his age to be near seventy five. His face was tired and gaunt. He also noticed the sunken cheeks, with muscles that looked as if they were wasting away. The paramedic continued, "He has a fractured radius. His blood pressure is dropping 105/50 and his pulse ox is well below 95%."

Nurse Hanson called out, "Arterial blood gases are clear."

As Dr. Johnson gently probed the man for injuries, he cried out in pain at the slightest touch near his left ribs. "Let's get this man's shirt off," he ordered.

As soon as the shirt was removed, Dr. Johnson knew what was happening. The right side of the patient's chest was rising markedly less than the left. When he was thrown from the car, he must have suffered not only from a rib fracture, but tore his pleura as well. Air has leaked into the lining of the lungs. The pressure was so great now that the right lung was no longer able to inflate, which in turn prohibited the heart from sending blood to the lungs, resulting in a tension pneumothorax. They must act quickly or the patient could also suffer cardiac arrest.

Nurse Hanson got Dr. Johnson's attention, "Dr. Johnson, the patient has a high fever. It is 106 degrees."

"We need to have the lab check for the virus, but first get me a decompression catheter."

Nurse Hanson called out, "Dr. Johnson, his stats are falling. His pulse ox is now at 75%. Do you want to intubate him?"

Shaking his head, he said, "No, this is a tension pneumothorax. I need to relieve the pressure right now. Unfortunately, if this poor man does have the virus, we will be doing all of this for nothing."

As he prepared for the procedure, he informed Nurse Hanson, "We need to call the cardiothoracic surgeon as well. There is a chance that he will need a chest drain."

Dr. Johnson found the space between the second and third rib on the right side. He then placed the twelve gauge needle in the upper border of the third rib and felt the skin break. As he applied more pressure, Nurse Hanson called out, "We are losing him."

As if in slow motion, Dr. Johnson pushed the needle deeper into the patient's chest. Instantly, a rush of air whooshed into the catheter's air bag, as it began to balloon out. He watched as the right chest wall inflated.

Nurse Hanson confirmed, "Blood pressure is rising and his stats are up to 85%."

As soon as the patient was ready for admission, the lab called with the results. Nurse Hanson looked over at Dr. Johnson with a grim expression, "The lab has confirmed that the patient does indeed have the virus."

Dr. Johnson had no time for depression to set in. The night was nothing more than a blur. An hour before he was to sign off, he learned that his patient passed away. The only good news that came out of the accident was that mother and baby were doing well.

Chapter 33

When Gregory Thompson walked into the president's office with a stack of papers, he saw the television was tuned to CNN.

Without looking away from the television screen, the President stated, "The press is reporting it as a pretty nasty strain of the flu."

Thompson found himself drawn to the television screen as well. "I still find it a miracle that the press is being so cooperative."

In the back of Thompson's mind he wondered if his own boss played an important role with regards to that. Blackmail was important in the press being contained. There was no other reason in his mind.

"We do have one reporter investigating the story relentlessly. So far he has been unable to prove his theories."

Without flinching, the President stated, "Let's keep it that way."

Chapter 34

It started out as nothing more than a sore throat. Fran Connelly tried to convince herself that it was a simple cold, but by morning, she knew that it had to be more than just that. She swore she could feel the heat from the fever cooking her brain.

Now, she wished she had called the moms earlier to tell them not to bring their children this morning, but it was too late. She would just have to push through this and do her best not to breathe on all the children. Thankfully, it was Friday and she only had three of her six children.

As she handed out French toast sticks to her tiny group, they were already arguing. "Miss Fran, his stick is bigger than mine."

Jake stuck his tongue out at Emma, "Stop being such a baby."

Emma immediately began to pout, "I am not a baby." Looking over at Fran she whined, "Miss Fran, tell him that I am not a baby."

Fran placed a French toast stick on Derrick's plate before replying, "Listen now, the two of you. If you keep up this bickering, I won't let you watch a movie this morning."

Emma immediately brightened up, "Can we pick out the movie, Miss Fran?"

"Yes, you can pick out the movie as long as you all behave."

No sooner than Fran finished plating their breakfast, the children finished their food. In unison, they showed her their cleared plates. "Look how good we ate, Miss Fran. Can we go watch the movie now?"

Forcing out the compliment she said, "I am so proud of you guys. You did really well." After cleaning their hands and faces, she escorted them into the living room. "Did you guys decide on a movie?"

Fran put the movie that Emma handed her into the DVD player and handed each of them a blanket. "Let's play lazy today. Miss Fran isn't feeling too well."

For a moment, Fran thought about calling her daughter to see if she could come over and help with the kids, but Amber needed her rest since her baby was due in a less than two weeks. The last thing Amber needed was to catch the flu from her mom. This would be her first grandchild and she could hardly wait to meet him.

Fran sat down in her own recliner and was immediately jolted by a vicious coughing attack. With each cough, a stabbing pain pierced her heart. Emma scooted herself off of the couch and peeked over the arm of Fran's recliner. "Miss Fran, are you okay?"

Ruffling the young girl's hair, she answered, "I am fine. Just feeling a little under the weather is all." She scooted the child back towards the couch. "Climb on back up there and watch the movie now."

Without warning, white hot pain shot through her. As she reached for the phone to call Amber, she lost control of her bodily functions. Fran could hear the children's cries, as the darkness mercifully washed the pain away.

Fran drifted in and out of consciousness as she was loaded into the ambulance and rushed to the hospital. She could hear someone say, "It's a good thing that one of the children knew how to call 911."

An overwhelming sense of fear washed over her, as she found herself drifting off into unconsciousness once more. She has never felt so sick in all of her life. She was extremely disoriented, as another wave of pain wracked her body.

She didn't understand why this was happening to her. She went in for her routine flu shot. This year, though, Medicare offered the shot for free, which was a godsend to her. One of the reasons she has to babysit is because money is especially tight.

Up until her diagnosis of Multiple Sclerosis over twenty years ago, Fran never once thought of her own health. It was not until she awakened with no vision in her left eye that she started worrying. She went from being what she thought to be a perfectly healthy person, to one whose health declined at an alarming rate.

If not for her husband and children, Fran wasn't sure if she could have handled the diagnosis, much less the changes in her health from the disease. She thought the exacerbations were bad, but she was now badly mistaken after this latest bout with the flu. She would gladly take an exacerbation over this flu.

The ambulance ride, even though she was in and out of consciousness, was intimidating. It didn't take long for fear to settle deep into the pit of her stomach. She watched as the IV pole and bottle swayed, as the ambulance sped down the road.

She wondered if she would be alright. Could this possibly not be just the flu, but the multiple sclerosis taking over another part of her body?

She tried to ask the paramedic if she would be okay, but the words did not form. It was as if her body was no longer able to follow the simple commands her mind gave it. Terror was followed by panic, as she realized something was terribly wrong with her. It was as if she was living a nightmare that she could not wake up from.

She no longer had the strength to keep her eyelids open as they became tremendously heavy once more. Her attempts to breath became pitiful, uncoordinated gasps. Whatever was happening to her was rapidly worsening. This was like no other flu she has ever heard of. The news had reported several deaths associated with a new strain of a virus. Could that be what she has? She prayed that what she had was not fatal.

Agonizing pain moved through her body, as the realization that she was dying swept over her. A ringing sound went through her ears, as her world began to spin. She could feel herself choking on the bile rising up in her chest.

Chapter 35

Amanda indulged in another spoonful of the white chocolate crème brûlée and held back a moan of ecstasy. After living on hospital cafeteria food and take out, the meal at this Italian restaurant was pure delight. "Are you sure you don't want to try the dessert? It is really good."

Her date, Hayden Carter, a pilot that she met recently at the airport, laughed. "No, I am sure; besides, I am enjoying watching you eat."

Laughing, she said, "Desserts are my weakness." She looked at him once more. She was glad that she took the risk and accepted his dinner invitation. "I have really enjoyed tonight. Work has been so crazy that I have had little time for myself."

"I must admit when I first saw you on the plane, I never would have taken you for a doctor." Hayden said.

Laughing, she agreed, "I get that a lot."

"So why the CDC and not in a big hospital or private practice?"

"My father died of Lou Gehrig's disease when I was twelve. When he was diagnosed with it, I instantly wanted to know what it was and after his death, I wanted to find out why no cure had been found yet. My mom said that even though I was little, I always wanted to know how things worked and if something was broken, I would try to find the best way to fix it.

"When I started studying Lou Gehrig's disease, I found out there was a whole world of viruses and infectious diseases out there. In a way, I hoped I would discover a virus or disease that no one had yet discovered. I even had dreams of grandeur, where I would be the one who found the cure. When the position became available at the CDC, I honestly didn't think I would get the job, but I prayed I would. "

"So, you aren't worried about catching one of the viruses you study?"

Shaking her head, she replied, "No, I make sure that I wear all the necessary protective equipment and take all the precautions."

Taking her hand to his mouth and kissing her wrist, he said, "It is a shame that you have to cover that beautiful body of yours. I bet if the patients could get a good glimpse of you, they would instantly start to feel better."

Just the simple touch of his lips on her wrist melted her. It has been so long since she had time for a date, and right now, she couldn't remember the last time she had sex.

Of course, these feelings may be because she was close to finishing her third glass of wine. She knew that she was being extremely talkative, but it didn't seem to bother Hayden. He seemed content to sit back and listen.

As she found herself jabbering on about her family and work, she stopped and smiled over at Hayden. "I am so sorry. I am not normally this talkative."

"There is no need to apologize. I find everything you have to say quite fascinating, as a matter of fact."

Protesting, Amanda stated, "You didn't take me out to dinner to hear about my work, and I haven't given you much of an opportunity to talk about yourself."

As the waiter cleared away the dessert dishes, she asked, "Would you like to have a drink at my house before heading home?"

"That would be lovely, thank you."

On the way out of the restaurant, Hayden offered Amanda his arm, which she gladly accepted. He opened the car door and waited for her to be situated before closing the door. She found herself falling for this man only after a short time.

Hayden slipped behind the wheel and started the car up. A smile formed on his face as the engine came to life. Amanda watched how he handled the car. "It has always amazed me how men can become so infatuated with a vehicle."

Hayden looked over at her, placed a hand over his heart and gasped. "A vehicle. This isn't just any vehicle. This is one of the finest automobiles ever crafted." It was after all a Mercedes CL 550.

Amanda watched as he lovingly caressed the instruments and steering wheel. She wondered what those hands would feel like on her body. Amanda could appreciate the luxuriousness of the car as she settled into the rich leather seat, but to be honest, cars never meant much to her. All she needed was something to get her from point a to point b.

The short drive to her house was silent; she was starting to doubt her invitation for him to come in for a drink. She honestly didn't know much about him, except he was good looking and an airline pilot. However, something about him made her want to pursue a relationship.

Once inside her house, she poured each of them another glass of wine. "I am sorry about the limited choices. I may have a bottle of vodka here."

Shaking his head, he replied, "Relax. I am more of a wine person rather than liquor anyway. Being a pilot, we have to watch our alcohol intake. The new regulations have made it too risky to overindulge."

As they talked about his work, she noticed that he had not made a move towards her. She began to wonder if there was something wrong with her. Amanda went to take Hayden's empty wine glass from him, when he pulled her down onto his lap. He reached up and removed the clip holding her hair, causing it to spill down her back. He tangled his hands in it and brought her lips to his. Amanda found her arms moving up to his neck – not wanting the kiss to end. She whispered against his lips, "I don't want to spend tonight alone."

Hayden looked up at her, his eyes glistened with desire. Once more he took her mouth in a gentle caress, her breath skirting his lips. Only when her mouth was compliant and willing, did he deepen the kiss, thrusting his tongue inside to dance with hers. They kissed with such passion that it ignited a spark deep inside of her. This was what she has desperately wanted, no needed, for so long. She pressed her body against his and desire coursed through her body.

She reveled in his touch as his hands tenderly cupped her jaw. His lips blazed a trail to her neck and shoulders. He unzipped her dress and moved his hands so gently down her body; the feeling of his hands touching her bare skin turned her insides to molten lava.

In one swift move, he stood up and carried her off to the bedroom. Once they were on the bed, he moved his attention to her breasts. He rained tiny kisses over each of them, cupping them in his hands to bring them closer to his mouth. His warm lips closed over one taut nipple. She moaned as she closed her eyes and let the sensations take over her body.   He suckled and nipped, constantly changing as to catch her off guard. Her hands grabbed the bedcovers as he turned his attention to her other breast, giving it the same tortuous attention.

His gaze was all heat and never has she seen such fire in a man's gaze. Pleasure vibrated through her, as his hands worked their magic. He felt warm and solid against her body. His movements were slow and steady. He felt so good inside of her, so right. She could feel herself going over the edge and into oblivion.

Chapter 36

Christopher Allen knew that there was a story here, a big story. Something didn't sit well with all these deaths as a result of the flu virus.

He has started a spreadsheet that listed the names, dates of birth and death of those he knew had succumbed to the virus. He found it strange that over ninety percent of those passing away from the virus were elderly. There were very few younger people catching the virus and dying, but of those, all seemed to have a low immune system.

Today, he planned to talk to several nurses and doctors, in hopes of finding out more information. They could no longer deny that the body count was rising. As soon as he began his search for other areas fighting this, he came across a news broadcast from Portland, Oregon. "Good afternoon. This is Randy Overton with Channel Ten news."

Christopher took notice that the young reporter was standing in front of a bustling hospital. This could indeed be what he has been searching for. "An outbreak of a deadly virus at St. Anthony General Hospital here in Portland, Oregon has residents on high alert. There are now over two dozen confirmed deaths and a dozen confirmed patients in critical condition at the hospital."

As Christopher listened to the reporter, he knew one thing for certain; this guy would cause a panic in Portland.

"Officials here at the hospital are taking precautionary measures at this time. Presently, there is no indication that this particular strain of virus is communicable. Hospital officials have confirmed that the Center of Disease Control has been contacted. A triage area will be designated here at the hospital for anyone in the community exhibiting symptoms. They ask that you seek medical attention at the first sign of flu-like symptoms, so that proper medical attention can be given."

At the end of his broadcast, Christopher could feel the anticipation building inside of him. His mind was reeling at the various ways to approach this story. First, he needed to see if there were other cities reporting any deaths from the virus.

By the end of the day, he was ready to call it quits. So far, he only had one doctor that would even talk with him. He scrolled through his emails once more, hoping that someone answered him back.

His phone rang and an unfamiliar female voice greeted him, "Christopher Allen?"

"This is he."

"I have some information for you. It is about the virus."

"Who is this?"

She replied, "If you want the truth, please meet me at nine o'clock tonight at Whiskey Haven."

Chapter 37

Amanda was finally starting to catch up on all the work she pushed aside for the influenza outbreak. Hayden called earlier today to let her know that he would be in Atlanta for a few hours tonight. They made dinner plans at one of the restaurants near the airport, since it was only a short layover. To avoid wasting any time, Amanda offered to pick him up at the airport. She warned him that her car was nowhere near as luxurious as his. With a laugh, he gave her his arrival time and gate number.

Each time the phone rang, she worried that it was Hayden calling to break the date, or worse that there was another rash of fatalities.

Amanda still has not found the cause of so many deaths with regards to this virus. She was trying to come up with a working hypothesis, but so far, the only commonality was the vaccine; unfortunately, the only sample she received from one of the clinics showed no contamination. There wasn't even a trace of the virus in the vaccine sample. It just didn't make sense.

In her spare time, she constructed a case map that depicted where each case was confirmed in the United States. There appeared to be no specific pattern that she could find, and that very thing was throwing her for a loop. She had compiled detailed profiles of the patients who have contracted the virus. The numbers were steadily increasing, so it was becoming harder to compile the data. Even though the sample she received was uncontaminated, she had a hard time dismissing the vaccine as the contact point for those patients who died or contracted the virus, since they all received the vaccine right before the onset of symptoms. She just wasn't able to prove the vaccines were contaminated.

***

Amanda wasn't sure just how long the phone was ringing when she finally answered it. The CDC operator's voice helped to wake her up. "I am sorry to wake you up, but I have an important call from Tuscaloosa, Alabama."

While the call was being patched through, she looked at the alarm clock and groaned. It was only three a.m. She has only been asleep for an hour and a half. If the call was coming this early in the morning, it must be because someone else needed help with the fatal influenza.

When she heard the doctor speak, she instantly knew that they were definitely dealing with a new location for the virus. "Dr. Bowers, my name is Dr. Jeremy Singleton. I must apologize for calling at such an early hour, but we have a serious problem here."

"I take it you had some deaths as a result of influenza."

"Yes, ma'am. We are hoping you can help. We are a charity hospital and there is a sudden influx of patients with the flu. What I don't understand is just about every patient that I am admitting reports they recently received their flu inoculation from this very hospital."

"Dr. Singleton, this is very important. Do you happen to have any of the vaccine left there at the hospital?"

"I believe so. We just received the package from the pharmaceutical company yesterday."

Amanda could feel her pulse quicken; she may finally be able to solve the mystery surrounding the flu and vaccine. "Please, do not inoculate anyone else with the vaccine until we test it to make sure that it has not been contaminated. Would you please also save the package and any instructions that came with it as well?"

"I will get right on it."

She started to look for a flight to Tuscaloosa. It took her a while, but she finally found a flight. The only problem was it left in forty five minutes. She quickly told Dr. Singleton that she would be there later that day and started getting dressed.

On her way to the airport, Amanda called the CDC duty officer to let him knew that she was leaving for Tuscaloosa immediately. "If you could please call Dr. Bentley and let him know what is going on, I would appreciate it."

"Consider it done. Have a safe trip."

Amanda found it almost unbelievable that the patients being inoculated at a charity hospital have now been infected with the influenza. If it wasn't the vaccine, it meant the pathogen more than likely was at the hospital.

Her flight was quiet with only a handful of passengers. When it landed, she was surprised to see a tall, robust man holding up a sign with her name. "I am Dr. Bowers."

Helping her with her luggage, he introduced himself, "I am Dr. Jeremy Singleton. As soon as I knew that you were on the flight, I knew that I had to meet you here. I was afraid you would have a hard time finding a taxi at this hour. Besides, we can use the travel time to get better acquainted."

"Have there been further admissions?"

Nodding his head, he grimly stated, "We have had thirty five deaths since I last talked to you and there has been another forty five admissions."

"Just how many patients did you inoculate yesterday?"

When he looked over at her, she could see the despair in his eyes. "Unfortunately, one thousand vaccines were sent to us. I went to get you one of those vaccines, only to find out that every last one has been used."

Amanda's shoulders slumped forward. She had hoped that she would have a chance to break down the vaccine to see if it indeed was contaminated. "So, you are telling me that you did indeed inoculate one thousand patients yesterday?"

"We offered a free clinic day where an abundance of patients came. I don't even think the nurses were expecting the influx of patients they saw. One of the nurses even commented that all they could remember were the forearms. They never had time to even look up to see the faces." Taking a deep sigh, he added, "One of the nurses did admit that she did not follow the standard protocol attached to the vaccine. She said that there were so many people there that they didn't confirm whether or not the patients had Medicare or Medicaid. She assumed if they were seeking medical treatment at a charity hospital that meant they couldn't afford treatment anywhere else, so she didn't see the harm in inoculating them as well."

Amanda looked over at Dr. Singleton. "The vaccine came with specific instructions?"

"I believe that is what the nurse said."

"Do you think that you can get me those instructions? I may be able to track down more information from this particular vaccine just by the letter. As far as I have heard, no one else has ever mentioned a letter being sent with the vaccines."

Excitement began to course through Amanda's body. If this particular letter did have any referencing batch numbers, etc., she may be able to find out more information. "We also need to look at the fact that the pathogen could indeed be at the hospital as well."

"I have already taken that into consideration. We are having everything disinfected and sanitized as we speak. There is not supposed to be an area of the hospital that has not been thoroughly wiped down at least twice. I even ordered the air ducts in the hospital to be thoroughly cleaned. The hospital administrator informed the cleaning and maintenance staff that he didn't want one area of the hospital that could not be eaten off of."

Once the car was parked, he turned to face her, "I must warn you that the hospital is in a state of panic. The hospital administrator is beginning to wonder if we need to just quarantine the entire hospital."

"Until we know for certain, I would suggest that you limit who you admit to the hospital."

"Unfortunately, it is not that easy. We are one of the only charity hospitals, and the surrounding hospitals are slow to see a patient they know will not be able to pay for the medical care. This is why we saw so many patients at the free clinic the other day."

As Amanda walked through the hospital, she was amazed that this was indeed a charity hospital. Even though the hospital was being thoroughly cleaned once more, she doubted that a pathogen could have thrived in these conditions. From what she has seen so far, the people who worked here cared very much for their workplace. Even though the equipment was old, it was not run down by any means. Everything was taken care of here with great pride. "I must say I am surprised with your facilities."

"We do the best with what we have. Just because the people we treat here cannot afford top medical care, does not mean that they should be seen in substandard conditions."

"I totally agree. I think more hospitals should look at your facility for inspiration."

Up on the isolation floor, Amanda took in the surreal state. The tiny floor was jammed with people, mostly patients waiting for beds. Dr. Singleton quickly explained, "We have limited beds. We are currently in the process of setting up cots and makeshift beds so that we can try to get these patients as comfortable as possible. I have already talked to several doctors at other hospitals who have treated patients with this virus. They all say the same thing; there is not much we can do, except to make the patients as comfortable as possible."

Amanda nodded her head in agreement. "Unfortunately, that is correct. I was hoping that with a sample of the vaccine we could confirm whether or not it was contaminated."

As they suited up to visit the patients, a nurse rushed over to them, "Dr. Singleton, here is the vaccine orders that you requested."

Dr. Singleton handed them over to Amanda. She let out a sigh. "I had hoped they would include a little more information."

The nurse nodded her head, "They were kind of generic. When I saw them, it almost reminded me of the instruction booklets you get with a table you have to put together."

Amanda slipped the instructions into her briefcase and finished suiting up. So far, she was running out of options on finding the pathogen causing the deadly virus. By the time they treated the patients, the virus was already dying.

As they finished suiting up to see the patients, a short, stocky man called out, "Dr. Singleton."

They both turned and watched the man make his way to where they were, "Mr. Stanley, I didn't expect to see you up here."

Mr. Stanley looked over at Amanda. "I heard a doctor with the CDC was here. I wanted to meet with her as soon as possible."

Amanda nodded to him, "I am Dr. Amanda Bowers."

"Dr. Bowers, I'm Hugh Stanley, hospital administrator. I wanted to thank you personally for responding so quickly, but I also wanted to apologize for the turmoil the hospital is in. We seem to have the beginnings of a panic on our hands."

"I am hoping that I can help you get some answers." She turned to Dr. Singleton, "Do you happen to have the blood test results?"

Dr. Singleton handed her a large folder, "We also have the results in each person's chart, but I thought you may want to see them all together as well."

Nodding her head, she opened the folder, as they made their way to see the first patient. Just by looking at the first set of results, she could tell instantly that this was the same fatal influenza the other hospitals were dealing with. "Do you know if any of your patients or medical staff has been to any of the other infected areas?"

"No, most of the people who are treated here don't have the money to travel. I can ask if anyone has had a recent visitor, but I doubt it."

Mr. Stanley chimed in, "Several of the medical staff are extremely worried they will catch the disease as well." Amanda felt for the man. It was one thing when you had unhappy patients, but when your professional staff was upset as well, it made for an extremely volatile mixture.

"I know that a lot of people are terrified right now. The only assurance I can give you at this time is that so far it does not appear to be a highly contagious virus."

"But, we have all of these presumed cases being admitted here."

Amanda nodded her head in agreement. "We are still trying to figure out just how the disease is spread, but so far, it does not appear to be through human contact." As Mr. Stanley went to remove his mask, Amanda stopped him. "That does not mean I would stop with the necessary protocol precautions. I would keep the patients isolated and wear the recommended gear. There are still just too many uncertainties with this disease."

***

Once Amanda saw the patients and reviewed the files, she called Dr. Bentley with her observations. "It is the same as the others."

As Amanda listened to what her supervisor was telling her, she began to feel progressively more unsettled. Once again, she had to inform a hospital in dire need of her help that at this time she was unable to help them.

She tried to let them down as easy as she could. "I am needed back at the CDC. It is felt that I will be able to do more good there than over here. They have the necessary equipment and a host of other available resources, which will help to ascertain how the flu is spreading." Amanda went on to tell the men, "We will continue working very closely with all the hospitals involved."

Dr. Singleton reminded her, "Yeah, and you still have not been able to find a cure for those patients either, have you?"

Shaking her head, she added, "Not as of yet." Looking him directly in the eyes, she stated, "We, or rather, I, have not given up."

 "Please do not think that we are upset with you. We all work for the same government and understand the bureaucracy that you are faced with. Trust me, we truly appreciate everything you have done and are doing for us. As a doctor, it is disheartening when you learn that there is nothing that you can do for your patient."

***

On the flight back to Atlanta, Amanda began the burdensome task of organizing the data. With so many patients involved this time, it becomes an extremely tedious task. This time, though, there were a few more constants than with the other patients. The most glaring constant of all was the fact that all the patients received the flu vaccine just before presenting with the symptoms.

Amanda pulled out the instruction sheet and studied it thoroughly for the first time. The nurse was correct in her assumption that it read similar to a generic instruction manual. For the life of her, she couldn't understand why this particular hospital received an instruction packet with their vaccines. That had her wondering if maybe the other clinics and hospitals received the same instructions as well. They didn't think of asking that question before. While it was still fresh in her mind, she sent a message to her secretary requesting that she start calling the various clinics and hospitals who were inoculating patients to see if they indeed received the same instruction sheet.

By the time she made it to Atlanta, she decided to go straight to her supervisor's office. After entering his office, she reported. "This one was worse than the others. The people there are so sick."

"I do not like to encourage your paranoid theory, but I am curious about the virus vaccine. This is simply too great of a coincidence. I trust that you will follow your instincts. Just be sure to err on the side of caution and exhaust all other possibilities, before you start blaming the U.S. government or even a pharmaceutical company. Both of these groups have very long arms and will not appreciate having the blame pointed at them." A moment of silence passed before he continued, "There is one more important thing you need to know; the lab has compared all the samples it has received and there is no doubt that they are all the same strain."

Once back in her office, Amanda looked down at all of her notes. The missing clue had to be somewhere in here. There had to be a commonality besides the virus.

Chapter 38

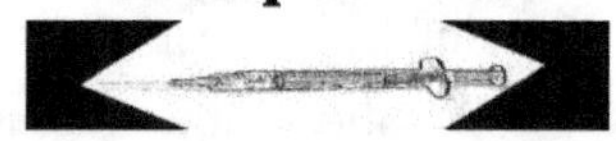

He looked across the street at his target. She was a lot taller than expected. She was dressed in a black pantsuit that clung to her very feminine form. She was calmly drinking her cup of coffee and didn't appear to be waiting for anyone.

Her demeanor was relaxed, almost to the point of perhaps being a little bored. The waiter stopped by to see if she needed anything, but she quickly waved him on.

Perhaps they have misjudged her, and she was still comfortable doing her job. What he saw was someone who had endless patience. She had not once glanced around at the patrons, nor did she look at her watch once. She didn't fidget with her hair or even attempt to make small conversation. She never once bothered to even check her phone.

As soon as she finished her drink, she dropped a tip on the table, picked up her purse, and walked off. She didn't turn to look back.

Thompson considered sending Kevin in to do this job, but he has fumbled too much lately to trust him with this detail; besides, she knew exactly what Kevin looked like and would more than likely bolt as soon as she saw him.

At one time, Kevin had been the most cunning and brilliant operative he has ever worked with. They have known each other going on fifteen years. There was not one physical characteristic that was memorable about Kevin, which made him the perfect operative. His features reminded you of the common man.

When he spoke, he never animated his voice; he always kept it purely monotone. His voice could even soothe a restless baby.

His forgettable face allowed him to blend in with those he met, except for those he saw on a constant basis. Thompson was certain that Miranda had memorized every small detail about the man's face.

He eased out of his car to follow her. For being down in the south, there was still a chill in the air, one that almost cuts you straight to the bone. He zipped his leather jacket as he kept his target in sight.

He has worked hard to achieve his position. The work, the sweat, the clawing to the top and he refused to allow anyone to ruin it for him.

He would not allow the walls he has carefully erected to come crashing down. There were too many secrets that could be revealed; secrets only their close knit group knew.

The four people, well five actually when you counted the mastermind, have all put their names to the decisions. They were some of the best minds in this country. They were all willing to work extra hours and do whatever it took to get the job done.

That was why Miranda must be taken out. There was too great of a chance that she would tell. Her boss, Randy Erickson, would be taken care of next. Intel showed that he was also planning to talk to someone, but unlike Miranda, he was for a much more tangible reward. Money.

Yes, telling secrets has always paid off big. It has been going on for as long as he could remember. He always kept his ear to the ground as well; besides, you could not expect to rise to the top if you didn't know which buttons to push.

As he was about to make his move, a movement near Miranda caught his eye. His eyes squinted to take in what he was seeing. For the first time in a very long time, he was actually thrown for a loop.

***

Kevin ran his hands along her smooth, naked thigh, up to her neck and then teasingly along her breast. Her body was pressed firmly against his, back to front. This was in no way part of the plan, but he had no complaints. There have been signs such as furtive glances and comments made in jest. The tension had been building with each meeting, as each of them silently wondered whether the other was thinking the same thoughts.

During their last meeting, he could see the desire in her eyes; there had been no hiding it. That was when he decided to make his move. He told her that they should no longer deny the sexual tension that was building between the two of them.

He nibbled gently on her bare shoulder; he felt the goose bumps forming along her body. He twirled a tendril of her silky hair and listened to her breath quicken. For a moment, he was completely intoxicated by the smell and touch of this beautiful, alluring woman lying next to him. He hasn't felt this alive in a very long time.

Guilt hovered in the recesses of his mind, waiting to come rushing forward at any moment. He could sense it gnawing at the edge of his psyche. He forced the guilt from his mind and reminded himself just what was at stake. Some things were better off forgotten. He came here to do a mission and it would be done.

Kevin has been able to excel at his job for the simple reason that he could stay twenty steps ahead of the enemy and everyone else for that matter. This ability has always kept anyone from being able to follow his way of thinking.

There was a reason why most professional killers typically came from Special Forces; they have been programmed to be desensitized to violence. Their missions were looked at as simply a way to achieve the desired end results. The solution was simple; they met violence with superior violence.

He learned long ago that killing a fellow human was easy. If you put someone in a live or die situation, their survival instincts would kick in, but if you gave someone hundreds of hours of training, they would kill without hesitation.

The human mind was easy to program, if using the right people. He found this out with his current mission. He learned how easy it was to program someone into easily killing an unarmed, innocent civilian. He has now moved into the role of executioner, not letting guilt cloud his mind. He was no longer killing a threat to himself, but learning a new skill, a killer without conscience.

Switching roles was easier than it should have been. He has now become the perfect, yet rare assassin, as have the rest of the members in their group.

Pulling himself away from her, he rolled onto his back and stared up at the ceiling. He was such a fool to think that he could even have a future with this woman. A family or a lover would give his enemies a tangible item to come after. Their lives would be forever threatened. He had too many enemies, too many relatives of people he has killed, too many government officials and powerful individuals who would like nothing more than to bring Jameson down a notch or two. They would think nothing of taking down a family member or lover to cause him despair.

No, he did not travel here to get romantically involved with this woman. He came here to make sure that she remained on board with all that was going on. He sensed the despair in her voice, even though she tried to hide it. He came here to kill her if need be.

It was sad that their sexual relationship was founded from a narcissistic politician who selfishly put his own personal needs above those of the American people. His scheming changed the course of America and has resulted in the deaths of tens of thousands of innocent people. With each passing day, it became obvious that they have actually gotten away with their plan. At this time, it was only their small group that knew just what was planned; unfortunately for this woman lying by his side, they could not let her disclose their involvement.

He has kept an eye on her and the others movements. They watched all of those who worked with the USAP closely;

they monitored their credit card and debit card transactions. Listening devices were placed in their homes, offices and even their cars. Their cell phones, as well as home phones, were closely monitored. Spyware was installed on all their computers and tracking devices on their cars. Jameson watched for a pattern to make sure that no one planned to leak any information.

The mission in front of him was simple; yet, there was no room for mistakes. They wanted it to look like an accident, but the solution in his eyes was simple; they need to let her fall prey to the very virus that was killing thousands of others. Another death would not cause anyone to even blink an eye, plus her death may help throw suspicion off of their current mission; besides with an accident, there was always a chance for questions to come to light. No, in his opinion, this was the only solution.

He looked at the woman next to him before he got up to pour them a drink. He already has the vaccine in her favorite coffee creamer. He learned one thing; Miranda was a creature of habit. With her obsessive compulsive disorder, it was easy to slip the poison into something. There was no visible pin prick to be found. It was easy to reseal the tiny package. He planned to simply pass her the cream at a morning meeting, but not this type of morning meeting.

He carefully slipped out of bed, covering her with the blanket. This assassination would be up close and personal. There was no detachment through distance. Even though his target was no match for him physically, this would be the most difficult kill for him. It would be the biggest psychological test he has ever been through. He would look her in the eyes as he poisoned her.

The woman he was getting ready to kill just felt the heat of his body, felt him inside of her and heard his moans of passion.

He prepared the small tray with an assortment of pastries he had room service send up as well as the coffee. He slipped her coffee creamer onto the tray and finished off the tray with a red rose.

He could hear her stir in the other room. It was time to set Miranda free from this world.

As he left the room, he made sure that the "Do Not Disturb" sign was on the door. By the time her body was found, the remaining members of USAP working on the case would have fallen victim to the virus as well.

Chapter 39

Christopher Allen may be playing the role of his life. He looked in the mirror once more and was happy with his appearance. It took a moment or two to get used to the mask, but otherwise, he was comfortable with the disguise.

With the current virus and the warnings of prevention all over the media, no one would give the gloves on his hands a second glance either.

He stopped by a local spy shop this afternoon and purchased a mini voice recorder and camera as well. In his ears, he has what appeared to be a simple hearing aid, but in fact, they were a special listening device, which could amplify those talking around him. If he was right and this story was big, the newspaper would be more than happy to reimburse him for his expenses.

In the Emergency Room, he sat down next to an elderly woman who was here by herself. Just from looking at her, he could tell that she was deathly ill. If anyone would look over at them, it would appear as if he was a loved one sitting and waiting for her to be seen.

He listened to the conversations around him, waiting to learn something that would lead him in the right direction.

His ears tuned in to a nurse asking those who were sick if they did indeed receive the free vaccine from Medicare or Medicaid.

He listened as the patient answered the questionnaire the nurse had. As he coughed heavily into his handkerchief, the nurse waited for him to catch his breath before asking another round of questions. From what the nurse was asking, it appeared that Dr. Johnson had indeed convinced the administration here that this current flu could have something to do with the vaccine.

What Christopher couldn't understand was why the Department of Health and CDC weren't crawling all over the place. This seemed to be the very kind of illness they would want to be involved with right away.

On the other side of him, an elderly woman was complaining to the person sitting next to her, "You know, at some point I realized that I was getting old and even started preparing for death, but now that there is a real chance that I am about to die, I find that I am not ready for it." She coughed deeply, the severity wracked her body.

She looked at the woman next to her. "It is probably just a simple touch of the flu, though, don't you think? Maybe I should have gone in a day or two earlier to get my flu vaccine."

A shudder of fear moved through Christopher. As a journalist, he tried to keep all emotions out of his work, but this time he found it hard to do. Looking around at all these patients, though, he couldn't help but be moved.

In the short time he has been here, the waiting room has doubled in occupancy. Medical staff moved through the hospital carrying clipboards with attached questionnaires.

He knew one thing; they didn't pay these poor people near enough for the work they do.

Chapter 40

Amanda woke up with a renewed determination this morning. Even though it was still winter, it was almost as if they were having an Indian summer this morning. She dressed in a lightweight sweat suit and headed out. She had been so busy at work these last few weeks that she wasn't able to run her usual course. As she made her way down her road, she reveled in the morning air. This was what she needed to help clear her mind.

Once home, she turned on the television as she went to take her shower. She has always found the quiet unsettling. In less than half an hour, she was showered, dressed, and back on the road to the CDC. By eight o'clock, she was entering her office. The first thing she did was check the fax machine to see if there were any new notices that may have come in overnight. Then checked the call log for any calls that came in, which she wasn't alerted to.

She was relatively surprised, but relieved at the same time, to find that it was indeed a quiet night. Her fingers were crossed and she could only pray that the virus outbreak was finally slowing down. With no new reports coming in, she wondered if she could breathe a little easier.

She was also finding it difficult to keep her mouth shut at the appropriate times. Dr. Bentley reminded her on several occasions that until she had proof she needed to keep her opinions to herself. She thought she was being selective in who she voiced her opinions to, but in this bureaucratic system she began to doubt there was such a thing as a confidant. She honestly thought she was doing a good job in searching for the pathogen, but now, she speculated if she was searching too hard for the truth.

She was never one to believe in conspiracy theories, but since this has all come to light, she suspected that there was more here than met the eye.

There were too many unanswered questions, and she has never liked having a problem she could not solve. The idea of more deaths as a result of this virus terrified her. She has seen these patients up close and personal. She has talked to the doctors and heard their concerns over not being able to treat them.

***

Amanda pulled into her driveway to find Hayden waiting for her. She ran into his arms. "You are just who I need to see."

Kissing her he asked, "I take it you had a bad day?"

Shaking her head, she replied, "No. It hasn't really been a bad day. It has just been depressing."

Hayden held open her front door and said, "I stopped by to see if you wanted to go out for supper."

Smiling, Amanda asked, "How about I cook supper for us? I don't get the opportunity to cook that often, but I do truly enjoy it."

Since Amanda didn't have much of a selection in her refrigerator, they take a quick detour to the grocery store. She picked out some nice size pork chops, fresh portobella mushrooms, Marsala wine, fingerling potatoes, and asparagus. Hayden also chose a nice bottle of wine that would pair well with supper.

As Amanda began to prepare the food, Hayden opened the bottle of wine. Without her looking, he also sets aside a special dessert he picked up for them on his way over to her house.

While the grill pan was heating, Amanda carefully seasoned the pork chops. Once the pan was nice and hot, she seared them. In another pan, she began to sauté the mushrooms in the Marsala wine. Hayden watched her in amazement. "I think you missed your calling. You should have become a chef."

Amanda let out a soft laugh, "My mom was always at the doctor or hospital tending to my dad. It became a necessity that I learn to cook."

"I can just image all of the dishes you must have cooked for them."

A shadow of sadness passed over Amanda before she continued, "Nothing as extravagant as you would think. Money was tight; most of our money was spent on dad's medicine and ever growing medical bills. Still, I learned how to stretch meals at an early age and make things taste better than you could have imagined." Laughing at a memory she started, "I remember mom buying a freezer load of chicken at one time because of the price. For pennies, she purchased probably enough chicken to feed us for a month. By the fifth day, my dad was tired of chicken, so I decided to reinvent recipes to use the chicken in a variety of ways. I learned that it did very well in spaghetti, as sandwiches, and all sorts of dishes."

"Hmm, I just may have to buy you a few pounds of chicken just so that I can see what kind of dishes you could come up with."

"Now that I have a more extensive culinary knowledge, I would welcome the challenge. Although, I must admit that back then I did really well. My dad stopped complaining about chicken and even went as far as letting me know which recipes we could keep in my collection."

Hayden took her in his arms, "You miss him very much, don't you?"

Nodding, fighting back the tears, she replied, "Yes I do. I think that is why I feel at such a loss right now. It is as if I am watching his death all over again. There was nothing they could do for him back then and there is nothing I can do for these patients now."

Chapter 41

Christopher looked at the computer screen blankly as he decided what his next move would be. He had to weigh his options carefully. He had to think about the most rational course of action. With so many lives at stake, including his, what he did next had to be beneficial. He briefly looked upward and prayed that he made it out of this alive.

He was honestly not ready to die. This case has made him aware of how extremely close he was to death's door. Since finding out about this story, the very thought of death kept creeping into his mind.

As if on cue, his phone came to life. His hand trembles for a moment, as he reached for. With a grimace, he answered, "Yes, sir."

Charlie Mayon bellowed over the phone, "Christopher, I understand that you are going to be working from home."

"Yes, sir. I am following up on a story and would rather do it here." What Christopher left out was he would rather not risk the lives of all those who worked for the Springport Watchman at this time.

"This particular story you are working on, is it the reason that I have been getting calls nonstop about a reporter of mine who is trying to do an undercover story about the virus outbreak?"

Christopher jumped up from his chair and shouted into the phone, "What the hell?" He automatically started pacing;

trying to figure out just how anyone knew what he was working on. "How did someone find out what I have been working on? I have been doing the research on this in private. No one, and I mean no one, is supposed to know anything. Just how the hell did they figure this out?"

 "Forget about that for a second. I want to know if there is some truth to what you are working on."

"If I were to tell you what all I have found out right now, there is a chance your life could be in danger. Hell, for all I know, your very life may be in danger just by talking with me."

Charlie scoffed, "Son, relax. This isn't the first time a story has landed me in hot water and it won't be the last. I am interested in why the powers that be are interested in squashing this story, though."

Christopher let out a deep sigh. "I am interested in finding out just how they know I am working on it."

"This is the United States Government we are talking about. I am sure they have all the sites monitored, and they are watching for anyone looking for particular key phrases, etc."

"What do you want me to do, sir?"

Charlie let out a soft chuckle, "Why, stay on the story, of course. This could turn out to be huge, for both the paper and you."

Chapter 42

Thompson stood in front of his boss's desk and waited for him to finish his review of the report. He hoped that he would simply skim over the report before shredding it, but of course, that wasn't how he liked to do things. No, his boss liked to read every word in front of him.

Of course, you don't become director of the CIA by cutting corners. The man in front of him also has a photographic memory and a hyper analytical mind. He was one of the most ruthless people he knew.

He flipped through each page carefully, watching for any little inconsistency. Preparing these reports had never been a strong suit for Thompson or Kevin. No, that skill was always left up to Miranda; she would run the numbers and make corrections where needed. That was no longer the case since Kevin surprised all of them by eliminating Miranda with complete ease.

Chapter 43

Thompson thought for a moment he was dreaming that he heard his phone ringing. "Yes, sir."

"The CDC doctor is asking a few too many questions. It is time to end this."

He conceded, "This whole affair is turning out to be a nightmare."

"It will all settle down once she is shut up. People are starting to consider her theories and we can't have that."

Thompson reminded him, "There is no real evidence left that can implicate anyone. As a precautionary measure, I am going to the lab tomorrow and cleaning house."

***

Amanda looked over the documentation in front of her once more. The meeting has been going on for over two hours now. As she stood in front of the large white board, she looked over her notes again. "I just don't understand this. All of these patients should have been given the same vaccine, but not everyone is having the same results."

One of the other members of her team spoke up, "Are you sure that the only common denominator is the vaccine?"

Amanda nodded her head. "I am positive, but it just doesn't make any sense. This vaccine has gone through extremely thorough diagnostics, as would any of the vaccinations. The studies all indicated that the vaccine had a ninety-nine percent effectiveness rate. None of the results mention any of the side effects, as those who have died experienced. As a matter of fact, the side effects were mild, almost nonexistent."

"Should we pull the vaccine?"

Amanda shook her head, "Right now, this is our only fight against the virus. If we pull the vaccine, how many more would die without it?"

"Do you think it is time to close the public buildings?"

She looked at the numbers in front of her. "So far, it does not appear to be affecting the general public. It appears to be only the elderly and those with a compromised immune system. If it wouldn't be that they all received the vaccination, I would wonder if they could have possibly caught the virus while at a clinic, but they all were treated at different places. No, the common denominator is most definitely the vaccine."

"Have you talked to the pharmaceutical company to see if they could pull the vaccine and make another batch that may not be contaminated?"

Amanda nodded her head. "That is already in the works. Unfortunately, it can take up to eight weeks for enough vaccine to be ready. They have expedited shipment from the warehouses and are working around the clock, but we can only hope it will be enough. So far, the batches that have been pulled have shown no signs of contamination and as far as we can tell from the tests, there is no way that the virus could have been spread through the vaccine."

***

As Amanda pulled into her driveway, she could already hear a glass of wine calling her name. All she wanted was to fix a nice hot bath, enjoy a glass, and unwind. She dropped her keys and purse on the entryway table and moved into the kitchen. As she made her way to the refrigerator, someone grabbed her from behind and jerked her head with such force that she wasn't sure how her neck didn't snap. Out of pure instinct, she reached up and gripped the assailant's arm. Even with all of the strength she could muster, she didn't have enough to loosen the man's grasp on her neck.

In the next instant, she felt her dress being ripped in half. Terror consumed her, as she began to fear that she was about to be raped. A knocking at the door distracted the man long enough for Amanda to lean forward. As he tried to pull her back towards him, she grabbed a knife from the kitchen drawer. Without blinking, she swiped the knife towards her attacker and felt the knife slice into her attacker's body.

There was a scream, "You bitch." Another man's voice called out to her now, "Amanda, your front door was open." For a moment, she swore she heard Hayden calling out for her.

Her attacker threw her hard against the kitchen cabinet. As her head split open from hitting the edge of the counter, she fell to the floor. Groggily, she saw the large man struggle with Hayden. Shaken, she tried to make her way to the entryway. If she could reach her car keys, she could hit the panic button.

On unsteady feet and blood dripping from the open wound on her head, she slowly made her way to the entryway. As soon as she hit the panic alarm, she heard the back door slam shut. Hayden came rushing to her. He pressed a kitchen towel to her head. "Amanda, look at me. Are you okay?"

"What happened?"

"I was hoping you could tell me. I came by to surprise you and got surprised myself. That man was one mean looking dude. I called the police, and they should be here soon."

"I don't even know where he came from. He grabbed me from behind when I walked into the kitchen."

Hayden assisted her into the living room, where he began to tend to her wounds. "I am no doctor, but I do believe that you are going to need stitches."

"Ugh, I do not want to go to the hospital. I have seen enough of those lately. If you don't mind, I have a medical kit in the trunk of my car."

"Are you planning on stitching up the wound yourself?"

Trying to nod, but finding that simple movement caused her excruciating pain she added, "If you are too squeamish, I can do it by myself."

"I don't know how much help I will be, but I take instructions well."

Once in the bathroom, he helped her clean the wound more. "You were really lucky that you did not get hurt worse than you are."

"And you, what the hell were you thinking charging at that man." Reaching up and rubbing her hand across his chin, "What if he had a gun?"

Shaking his head, he replied, "To be honest with you, I wasn't planning on being a hero of any type; I just acted. I didn't see a gun in his hands when I entered and was hoping I had the element of surprise, but I think you beat me to that, too. We were both surprised when the knife slashed across his face."

"All I could think of was I didn't want this guy to rape me. When I heard the dress rip, I knew I had to do something. If you hadn't knocked when you did," a shiver ran across her body, "I don't know what would have happened."

In the distance, they heard the sound of police sirens approaching. Amanda looked at Hayden, "So much for this being a pleasant surprise."

The police car pulled up to her house with lights flashing. Two uniformed policemen walked up to her door and looked around before entering. "Did you notice anything out of the ordinary when you got home?"

"No, I didn't."

As their line of questioning continued, Amanda found them not only sensitive to the way they asked the questions, but efficient as well. They refused to listen to her protests and had an ambulance dispatched to the house. The officer told her, "I would feel much more comfortable with them looking you over; even though I am sure you are an excellent doctor. Besides, the crime scene techs will be busy for a while here gathering evidence and dusting for prints."

Amanda asked, "Did you figure out how he even got in here?"

The other officer explained, "You really do need to look into upgrading your locks. They are very easy to jimmy. It only takes a matter of minutes to unlock the door with the right equipment."

"This has always been a safe neighborhood, though. I don't think I have ever heard of any problems here before."

"Unfortunately, there is no such thing as a safe neighborhood anymore. With the economy the way that it is, crime is on the rise."

While the paramedics examined Amanda's injuries, the police officers continued asking questions. The only problem was that neither Hayden nor Amanda had gotten a really good look at the intruder. At the time, Amanda wasn't even sure if anything was missing.

Almost two hours later, the police left. With tears in her eyes, she told Hayden, "I am so sorry about all of this."

He pulled her in his arms and gently hugged her., "There is nothing to be sorry for. I am just glad that I was able to be your hero tonight."

Once inside, Amanda couldn't stop shaking. "What time do you have to go back to work?"

"My next flight isn't until tomorrow afternoon. I actually have a fairly long layover."

"I don't know if I can spend the night here. I am going to jump at every noise."

Hayden pulled her to her bedroom and said, "Well then, let's pack you a bag and you can spend the night at my house." He stopped her before she could object, "No objections. I won't be able to rest knowing that someone just broke in here."

Chapter 44

The interior of the bar was dim, too dark to see anything clearly. If you wanted a clandestine meeting, this was definitely the place for it. Christopher Allen strained his eyes to make out the figures in the room.

He was fairly certain it was a woman who called, but voices could be deceiving over the phone. As he looked around, the door opened and a woman walked in.

***

Jessica Lathrup looked around the room, hoping to spot the news reporter. From the way she was looking around, this must be the person he was meeting. He got up to greet her, "I believe you may be looking for me."

For a moment, her heart caught in her throat. This man was not what she expected. He had a very powerful presence. His dark brown eyes were piercing. He was clean shaven, except for his goatee. He stood well over six feet tall and was built like a linebacker. She has never been one for men with long hair, but on him, it looked damn sexy; although, she supposed men didn't consider hair that hit right above the chin long anymore. "Christopher Allen?"

"Yes."

Jessica was anxious to get this meeting started, so she stated, "Let's find a table in the back."

Chris took her elbow and escorted her to the back of the bar. She looked at him with relief in her eyes, "I was afraid you wouldn't come."

"This is an interesting meeting spot."

Shrugging her shoulders, she said, "At least it is dark and there is a back exit if we need to escape."

Taking out a tape recorder he asked, "Do you mind if I record our conversation?"

"No, go ahead. This whole thing is a mess anyway."

"From your accent, I take it you are not from here."

Jessica shook her head, "No, I am not from here. You were asking questions in the medical community that has certain people interested in you. You should be very careful, because there are some people that do not want the answers known." Jessica looked around the room, "I tried to meet with a friend of yours, but he was too hard to get to. They are watching him closely. I need you to pass a warning on to him as well."

"And just which friend is that?"

"Dr. Johnson is getting too curious and my supervisors are not happy with his line of questioning. He and some of his associates are close to discovering the answer and they cannot let that happen."

Chris looked at her and asked, "And if I need to get in touch with you?"

"After I leave here, you will not be able to find me. Now that my supervisor knows that I am actually missing, he will begin to put the pieces together rather quickly. My life is already over, but before they can silence me, I need to pass this information on to you. If I give it to the doctor or CDC, I can't guarantee that the public will find out the truth, but with you being a journalist, I know that my death will not be in vain."

"Surely, you don't believe that you are going to die?"

Jessica tried to hold back the tears threatening to spill, "As soon as I took the sample, I knew that my time on this earth was done, but I could not live with myself if I did not do something about what was happening." Jessica took in a deep breath. "I work for a government agency that few know about. I am a secretary with the Unacknowledged Special Access Project department, otherwise known as the USAP. The Unites States Government uses us to control sensitive research programs. Normally, my job is very boring, until I happened to notice my boss being more and more secretive. The security there is always high, but when Miranda started doing her own secretarial work, I knew something was up. I also overheard one day that they were testing prisoners for a new vaccine. Now, that is not normally something that we would be involved in at all, so I did a little snooping and found out something that made my blood run cold. They had been using prisoners to indeed do trial runs on a vaccine, but this vaccine was not meant to prevent the flu; in fact, it was meant to kill anyone who was inoculated with it."

Chris looked up at her with surprise showing on his face. "You are saying that the United States Government actually wants a vaccine that will kill these people?"

"What I am saying is the Unites States is in desperate need to control the deficit. It appears that there are a few select members of the government who found a way to do that."

"Okay, but if it was just to decrease the numbers in prisons wouldn't it have been easier to just poison everyone there? Surely, a poisoned vaccine is a little overkill, don't you think?"

Jessica shook her head. "No, the prisoners were the government's lab rats. Have you ever noticed just how many people are on Medicare and Medicaid? Every month, millions of dollars are paid out in Disability and Social Security. There are those in the government that feel as if these people have outlived their usefulness."

"So, are you saying that the government has taken it upon itself to develop a vaccine that will basically kill off those it feels are a drain on the economy?"

Jessica nodded her head in agreement. "That is exactly what I am saying."

"But, surely someone higher up would have found out about this and stopped it?"

"I am fairly certain that this particular order came all the way from the top."

Chris ran his hand through his hair before asking, "Wait a second. You honestly believe that the President of the United States gave the order for this to happen?"

"Let's just say I know he did. My boss is very obsessive compulsive. She keeps a hard copy of everything she does in a spot she believes is hidden. I have taken pictures of everything she had in there."

Jessica reached into her purse and handed Chris a flash drive. "This is for you. I trust that you will make sure the public knows about this."

When the bar door opened, Jessica knew instantly who it was. Just from the shape, she knew that he had found her. The hair on the back of her neck rose as he walked into the dimly lit bar. That was a sure sign that something wasn't right. She had changed the color of her hair in an attempt to throw him off guard. She even purchased a cheap pair of reading glasses to alter her appearance even more.

An uncontrollable urge to laugh took over her. Two weeks ago, she had a normal life; hell, even a week ago, her life had been somewhat normal. She should have listened to her grandmother, "Curiosity killed the cat." She learned the hard way that simple statement held so much truth to it. If only she hadn't been so curious.

Once she discovered what they planned, though, she couldn't stand idly by and do nothing. If only she had found out sooner, how many more lives would have been saved?

***

Chris could actually see Jessica blanch when the man walked in. She pulled him out of his chair, "We have to go now." As they were leaving, she slipped him another package. "This, you have to be very careful with. This is the only vial I have of the vaccine. You must make sure that it gets into the right hands."

As they made their way out the back exit he asked, "Where are you going?"

"I don't know, but I am going far away. It is not safe for me here. Now that he has seen you with me, it is not safe for you as well."

As she was pulling away from him, he grabbed her arm, "Wait, I think I know a place where we can both get a good night's sleep and discuss this some more."

Jessica shook her head, "It is too dangerous to go back to your place. I am fairly certain that by now they have your place under surveillance and more than likely your doctor friend as well."

Chris pulled Jessica close and whispered in her ear, "Dr. Johnson is no longer staying at his house. He moves from hotel to hotel; he is paying in cash to keep his whereabouts hidden. He is already concerned about his safety."

"So then where do you suggest we go?"

Chris asked her, "How did you get here?"

"I have a rental car, but I am sure that they have already found it."

"You are more than likely correct. Do you have an extra change of clothes?"

"I put all my items in a locker at the airport before heading this way. That way, if I did need to ditch the rental car, I would still have my belongings."

"Good, let's go collect your items, and I will put you up for the night."

Jessica shook her head vigorously, "No, you don't have to do that. It is too dangerous."

"Look, we don't have to go to the airport tonight to get your stuff if that will help you feel safer, but please allow me to put you up some place safe."

 "You are sure that we will be safe?"

"Yes, I am certain."

***

Kevin followed Jessica and the man out of the bar. He ducked into a shop just as Jessica glanced behind her. Seconds later, he emerged only to find that they were gone.

Kevin's chest tightened and his hands clenched. He let out a silent curse. There was no way that they could have gotten away this quick. He broke into a fast paced walk.

As he rounded the corner, he perused the street for them; unfortunately, the street was devoid of life. This couldn't be the way that they had come. There was nothing here but small boutiques and an occasional café. He smashed his right hand into the palm of his left hand, as rage enveloped him. He could feel his face turn a scarlet red, as he tried to force himself to calm down.

He reminded himself that he must be patient. If he has learned one thing over the years, it was patience was a virtue. Mistakes happened when you let your emotions take over.

***

Once they were certain that they had lost their follower, they slowed down, but they did not let their guard down. The reality that they were caught in a dangerous web of conspiracy and intrigue was almost too much to believe. Now that the exhilaration of escaping their pursuer was fading, Jessica noticed how clear the night was for the first time. It was beautiful, with only a fragment of a moon and stars piercing the black velvet sky, twinkling like diamonds up above.

The night air was cool enough to make her shiver, or could it be from fear? The fear was still palpable, as they made their way to find a place to sleep for the night. Shaking her head once more, she wondered just how long she did had left on this earth.

As soon as they were in the hotel room and Jessica was sure that she was safe, the tears exploded. Chris wrapped his arms around her. He continued to hold her, rocking her back and forth, until the fierce sobs no longer wracked her body.

Moments passed before she was able to calm herself once more. She breathed in deeply, re-centering herself. Her cheeks were flushed and she found herself unable to look into his eyes. When she finally looked up at him, he could see the fear still there in her eyes. "I am so sorry."

Christopher gently brushed her hair back before replying, "There is nothing to be sorry for."

She nodded her head. "I have put your life in danger."

As he bent down to kiss her, she pushed back, "Wait."

Jessica told him, "I don't know if we should get involved. I feel as if my days in this world are numbered. It wouldn't be fair to you to start a relationship..."

Cutting her off, he pulled her tightly against his body. He buried his face in her hair. "I will take my chances."

"I am not sure I am ready for a relationship, but if you are willing to take a chance, I am tired of wishing I had what other people have..."

He put a finger over her lips, "Shhhh, you talk too much."

She looked up into his face. He continued, "I will take it slow if you want, but I will not leave you alone to deal with this. No matter what happens, I will be here at your side."

Slowly, incrementally, her face moved closer to his. Her eyes closed, as Christopher tangled his hands in her hair and brought his lips to hers. Her breath caught in her throat from the simple touch of his lips.

She moved in closer to his body. She tried to imprint the feel and smell of him in her memory. He whispered in her ear, as he cupped her face, "I could get used to this." He took her lips in his once more.

Chapter 45

Dealing with arthritis and the damn multiple sclerosis, they were perfectly synchronized to make his life a painful living hell. What a perfect duo to accomplish that!

Every bone in John's body creaked; every muscle in his body ached. Any movement sent a shooting pain throughout his body; yet, he forced himself to keep going, because if he stopped it would be for good.

He downed his newest potent cocktail of prescription medication the neurologist had him on, grabbed his sunglasses and headed to his car. As he eased out of the driveway, he went over his grocery list once more.

His only plans for today was going to the VA Clinic for his free flu vaccine andto the grocery store, before grabbing a bite to eat, and once again heading home.

As he found a parking place at the VA Clinic, he was surprised to see just how many people were here already. He thought for sure arriving at seven thirty in the morning it wouldn't be busy. But it looked as if everyone else had that very same idea.

As he stood in line waiting for his turn, he thought of just how fortunate he was. He had no money worries; Uncle Sam has been very kind to him. Before being diagnosed with MS, he was serving year sixteen in the United States Marine Corps.

Now, he not only has his medical retirement from the military, but one hundred percent VA benefits as well as social security disability. He also received first rate health care at the local VA hospital, all thanks to Uncle Sam.

As in previous years, the flu shots have been always free of charge, but this year, the only difference was the clinic was requesting they be inoculated by a certain date. John figured they must be concerned about a shortage this year.

By the time he left the grocery store, he began to feel a little under the weather. He had really wanted to stop by his favorite deli, grab a sandwich and flirt with the pretty waitresses. Now, all he wanted to do was go home and crawl into bed.

Little did John Sinclair know that his life was about to end. He was to become yet one more statistic.

Chapter 46

Amanda arrived at the office early, despite her harrowing experience last night. As soon as she was seated at her desk, Jane walked in. "Dr. Bowers, what on earth happened to you?"

Not wanting to go into detail about what happened last night she said, "I had a little accident is all."

"Well, that doesn't look like a little accident. I came in to tell you Dr. Bentley asked that you come to his office right away."

As soon as he saw the injury on Amanda's head, he knew that the rumors were true, "I received a call late last night informing me that you were attacked in your home earlier. I was even told that it would be in everyone's best interest if you were offered some vacation time so that you could recuperate."

Amanda looked at him with surprise. The only ones who knew about the attack were Hayden, the responding officers, and the paramedics. "I appreciate the consideration, but to be honest with you, work will keep my mind occupied."

"I agree, but I also think that you need to tread very carefully right now. I received another phone call early this morning. I do believe you are starting to ruffle some feathers, my dear. A certain Congressman, a senior member of the House Appropriations Subcommittee for the Department of Health and Human Services, called to make sure that I offered you a paid vacation in light of your accident."

That very comment left Amanda speechless. "Just how did anyone know that I was attacked?"

"That, my dear, is the million dollar question, but more disconcerting is why a Congressman even called with regard to a CDC doctor?"

"And are you going to listen to the direct order that I take a vacation?"

"My dear, that is solely up to you. On one hand, I am sure that you do need the time off with regards to your head injury, but then again, we also need your help with regards to the influenza outbreak. A few more cases popped up overnight; these were nothing as extreme as what we have seen, but I am worried it will only be a matter of time. If you do take a vacation, we need to make sure someone else is fully apprised of the situation."

"Well, you can put your mind at ease, because I have no plans on taking a vacation. I am also beginning to suspect that someone does not like my line of questioning."

"Yes, but how is it that they know about your line of questioning? I, for one, have not breathed one word of this to anyone."

Amanda was suddenly overwhelmed with fear. The attack in her home wasn't just a crime of opportunity; someone had actually tried to kill her. What could she know that inflicted such fear in someone to result in wanting her dead? If her assumptions were true, then this could be a conspiracy of immense proportions and her life was in extreme jeopardy.

Suddenly, she had a feeling that she was in way over her head, but who could she trust? She was starting to believe that this was definitely a conspiracy of some sort, but she was unsure as to what extent and just how high up this conspiracy went? Her main problem rested in the lack of proof that the vaccine was causing the fatal flu epidemic. All she had right now was highly suggestive facts.

There was no doubt in her mind that whoever had contaminated the vaccines had some very powerful connections, but why would someone do this? Why kill all of these people? It seemed that if another pharmaceutical company wanted to hurt their competition, they would have instantly harped on the deaths; but also, they would immediately announce that their vaccine was better and definitely safer.

She just had no idea how deeply someone with the CDC was involved in this.

Chapter 47

Dr. Johnson rolled over in the dark hotel room and smacked the alarm clock. It took him a moment to remember just which hotel he was sleeping in. He was fairly certain that someone was tailing him and he refused to give them a chance to catch him by surprise. Working nights, it was harder to sneak around, but he was finding ways of doing just that.

On his way to the hospital, he picked up a coffee and a bagel. The hotel he was currently staying at was only a few blocks from the hospital, so he was able to walk there. More than likely, he could only stay there a couple more nights before his location was again discovered. He planned on playing it safe. It could be that he was being overly paranoid, but his gut kept telling him his life was in danger. His only safe place was the hospital; there were just too many witnesses there.

Once outside, the humid air hit him. Although the temperature outside was pleasant, the humidity remained high.

As soon as he saw the line in the ER, he knew that it would be a very long day. The line was almost to the street. As he made his way inside, he tried to mentally count the people waiting. At a glance, it appeared to be right around thirty people just in the line outside.

Inside it was filled to capacity. People were lying and sitting on every surface they could find, some were even on the floor. It reminded him of a scene you would expect to see in a third world country and not here in the United States. It wouldn't be long before the staff was once again overwhelmed.

As the numbers increased, he feared they would see more people panicking. Most of those who were ill would eventually seek medical treatment, and with the increasing lines, the waiting time would become greater. It wouldn't take long before the city exploded with fear. Above all else, they must try to keep that from happening.

He passed Nurse Landry, as she brought a wheelchair to a patient, "Good evening, Dr. Johnson. We are almost out of wheelchairs."

"Evening Sharron. It looks as if it will be a busy night."

She nodded and continued on with her patient. Inside, the nurses looked even more frazzled than yesterday. Nurse Hanson called out to him as soon as she spotted him, "Dr. Adams asked that you start seeing patients as soon as you come on. He said that he will stay a little later today to help you triage most of the ill."

"Has it been like this all day?"

Nurse Hanson nodded her head, "It has been a steady influx of patients."

"How are we on beds?"

With a grim expression she explained, "Unfortunately, most of those who were admitted yesterday have already passed away."

He nodded and patted her arm before moving on to see patients. He took notice that today there seemed to be more elderly women than men, very few younger adults and no children. The hospital had a heavy disinfectant smell, but even that strong smell did little to hide the smell of sickness and death that emanated from the patients.

All around him, he noticed the yellow, vacant eyes staring out into nothing and the shallow breathing that only confirmed that these patients were at death's door, as hopelessness clung to them like a shroud. He wondered if something sinister was at work here. There were just so many sick, and they were mainly the elderly.

As he read one of the patient's charts before stepping into the room to exam him, depression set in. The poor man had already passed away. He gently closed the man's eyes and covered him with a sheet. After he placed the red toe tag at the end of the bed, he cleaned up to treat the next patient.

The hospital had already admitted almost three times the number of patients as yesterday. As soon as Dr. Adams saw him, he walked over. "I am glad you came in early."

"You should have called. I would have come in earlier."

Shaking his head, he said, "I knew you were going to need your rest. I am already dead on my feet, but I want to see if we can catch up."

Dr. Johnson surveyed the patients, "There are so many new patients."

Dr. Adams informed him, "The nursing homes have called. They are dealing with the same thing there. Bill sent over a team to each nursing home, instead of having the patients come here."

"I take it that team will work there for the duration?"

Dr. Adams nodded his head, "It would be easier that way. Until we find a cure for this thing, there is no way we can keep up with the influx of patients; however, it does mean that we will have to pull even longer shifts now since we are short staffed."

"Not a problem." Dr. Johnson could see the worry lines and fatigue on his face. "We are all doing the best that we can do."

"Unfortunately, that isn't much. In reality, all we can do is try to keep the patients comfortable until..." Instead of finishing the sentence, his voice drifted off. Dr. Johnson was starting to realize that underneath that hard exterior Adams displayed, he really was a compassionate doctor.

The magnitude of what they were dealing with hit him when he walked into one of the rooms set up with the critically ill. Nurses were giving the patients sponge baths in an attempt to cool off their fevered skin. They were making sure ice chips were available to help with dehydration and pain pills were readily available to those who asked.

Picking up a chart, he stated, "Hello, Mr. Aucoin. Dr. Adams is getting ready to head home. My name is Dr. Johnson and I will be taking care of you."

Instead of answering, he just stared up at the ceiling with a vacant look. "Can I get you anything?"

He shook his head once and fell back sound asleep, as if that simple movement had been too much exertion for his sick body.

It was difficult not being able to treat patients. In between patients, he walked into the morgue to see just how many have passed away recently. His mind reeled in horror as he looked around. The morgue was wall to wall gurneys of the recently deceased. Some of the bodies were misshapen and twisted by the terrible pain they endured.

He swallowed hard, fighting down the sudden surge of bile that formed in the pit of his stomach. With trembling hands, he walked back upstairs to try and save those who were still alive.

***

Nurse Sally Hanson moved slowly through the room. Her feet were heavy as she tended to the sick. There were so many patients now. There were more than she could have ever imagined.

She tucked askew legs and arms back under the blankets, and she tried to comfort as many patients as she could. All around her was moaning, violent coughing, and cries.

Some of these patients she knew personally. It was so hard not to let all these deaths get to her.

Chapter 48

As he drove down the interstate, he thought about what his life has become. Technically, it wasn't much of a life; he wished he had never been forced to retire. His gaze discreetly eased in all directions. He has yet to overcome the impulse to check and see if he was being followed. Of course, you get that way when people were always trying to kill you, but what he did for a career beat the hell out of some nine to five miserable day job. Over the decades, he visited different countries every month. Every month, he saw a different area of the world. Nostalgia fueled a smile, as it formed across his face. He had so many memories he could share, if only he could write a memoir of all his missions.

***

Kevin watched as his current assignment drove to his destination. The old man must be losing his observational skills now that he was stateside. He has yet to notice Kevin following him these last few days.

This man was predictable and that made him an easy target. Every day at six o'clock, he drove over to a local bar for a quick beer, flirted with the waitresses, and headed back home to read his newspaper in his backyard. He went inside for supper, watched TV for a short period of time, and played solitaire on his computer until going to bed. By eleven o'clock, he was sound asleep. Each day, he woke up to start the same pattern all over again. Kevin prayed that when it was his time to retire, his life was not as threadbare as this.

It only took Kevin two minutes to complete his task. The sticky residue containing the virus had been easy to apply to the car door handle. No one noticed when he leaned in close to the car door.

***

As Brian Mathis prepared his supper, he began to feel ill. Suddenly, he found it difficult to breathe. Something was terribly wrong. At first, he feared it was a heart attack, but there was no shooting pain down his arm and no pressure in his chest. It couldn't be a stroke either. His face didn't feel as if it was drooping, and he still had the ability to function. His mind raced as to what could be wrong.

He then remembered the sticky substance on his car door handle. It had been very greasy, and no matter how hard he would wash, he could not get his hands clean. It took several hand washings before he finally felt his hands were clean. Then it hit him, he had absorbed something into his body from his door handle.

His last thought before death was why and who would want him dead. Then he knew. He knew too many secrets, secrets that could end political careers. His job had never involved normal missions. It involved extraordinary missions, missions that some would never want made public.

Chapter 49

Dr. Johnson was getting ready to leave when a text message came in. "We need to talk. One hour at Victor's Cafe."

Thankfully, Victor's Café wasn't far from the hospital, but the last thing Johnson wanted to do right now was talk to anyone, even if it was Christopher Allen. Something in his gut told him that Christopher Allen may have found out some information.

At this hour of the morning, Victor's Café was the only shop open on the street. The other retail establishments wouldn't be open for several more hours, which was likely why Christopher had chosen this place.

Christopher was already sitting at a back corner table, but this time there was a very attractive woman with him. Dr. Johnson sat down as Chris informed him, "I already placed an order for us. I hope you don't mind."

The small café was one of the only places left here that had kept the interior design as close as possible to its original opening almost a century ago. The brick walls gave warmth to the place, while the photos of Springport through the years told the town's story.

The smell of coffee and scrambled eggs made your mouth water. The waitress brought over mugs of steaming hot coffee and a plate of fresh biscuits with fresh strawberry jam. With a practiced hand, she also laid out three nice size slices of ham and cheese quiche for each of them. "Here you go. Can I get y'all anything else?"

The hot, addictive scent of the food was thick in the air. Johnson thanked her as he looked around the room once more. The dining room was relatively empty at this hour. There was an elderly couple enjoying a platter of scrambled eggs and grits, a young man reading a book with a pair of earphones plugged into his ears, and a gentleman reading the paper in another far corner.

Christopher and the mystery woman sat quietly for a few minutes, as they all sipped their coffee. Johnson was starving, so he took a bit of the quiche and almost moaned in delight. The warmth of it filled his mouth. The quiche was light and fluffy, but packed full of flavor. In front of him was nothing short of a masterpiece. "You made a good choice with breakfast. I have been up all night working. This hits the spot for sure."

Christopher looked over at the woman and said, "I would like you to meet Jessica Lathrup. We had a very interesting conversation the other night; a conversation that I believe you will find useful as well."

"Miss Lathrup, it is nice to meet you."

Jessica gave him a tired smile. "You may not say that after you hear what I have to say."

Johnson looked over at Christopher. "I take it you are making some progress with your story?"

"I am making more progress than I ever hoped."

Before Christopher could elaborate, Jessica whispered to him, "I think it is time for all of us to leave."

For the first time since their arrival, Christopher now noticed that she was directing his attention to a rather tall man sitting in a black coat several tables away. He never once moved the newspaper he was reading, but every now and then, he took a quick glance over their way. "Do you know him?"

"I have seen him meet with Miranda a few times."

Johnson looked over towards the man, as he set his coffee mug down. "That is the man from the hospital. He questioned me not long ago on just how much I knew about the virus."

Jessica informed them, "I think he is one of those calling the shots."

Christopher pulled out some cash from his wallet, making sure to leave a hefty tip. "I think it is time to get out of here."

Johnson informed them, "I think our best bet right now is to stay out in the open. The streets are almost devoid of life right now."

Christopher asked, "Where do we head to?"

Johnson replied, "The hospital is our best bet. There is too much activity going on there for him to make a move there."

As they made their way down the street, Jessica whispered, "He is following us."

As they picked up their pace, a few more people finally started to appear on the streets. As they turned the corner, Jessica stopped and stared at the long line of people in front of the hospital. Her hand went over her mouth, silencing the whimper that threatened to escape. There has to be at least two hundred sick people waiting to be seen. Over ninety percent of those standing in lines were elderly. Their faces looked vacant and withdrawn.

As soon as they walked into the hospital, Johnson led them to the cafeteria. It was too busy here this morning for the man to try anything; unfortunately, they wouldn't have much privacy either. "Okay, just what the hell is going on?"

Christopher informed him, "Your theories weren't far off the mark. The vaccine is causing the deaths. Jessica gave me all the information I need to break the story."

Jessica stated, "That is if you live long enough to write it. I told you that I should have gotten the hell out of here. He will continue looking for me and not be worried with you."

Johnson shook his head, "I don't think so. I was run off the road not long ago, and I don't think they have stopped trying to hunt me down. I have not been back to my house since they tossed it, but something tells me that this man won't give up."

Jessica nodded her head in agreement. "There is too much at stake. They do not know what information I actually have, but I know that they don't want me talking to anyone." Letting out a sigh, she added, "Now that you have been seen with me, you are definitely a liability."

Christopher asked Johnson, "How well do you trust that lady with the CDC?"

"She seems to be genuine in wanting to find a cure for what is happening. Why?"

"I have something that I think we need to get to her as soon as possible; however, what I have must make it to the correct hands and not be disposed of."

Johnson looked over at the two of them, "Just what is it that you have?"

Jessica looked up at him, "The vaccine that is killing everyone, along with the notes that went with it."

Johnson ran a hand over his face. Could it be true? Could he be standing right next to the very vaccine that has caused so much death? Jessica informed them, "We need to let the proper channels know immediately what is happening, but we need to make sure that they are not working for the very same group I am running from."

Johnson asked, "How do we know that?"

Jessica looked up at him grimly, "That is the problem; we don't know. We have to trust that the person we give this to will help us. I have a feeling that they are getting ready to speed up the rate of inoculations. Now that they know it works and there is a chance their secrets may be exposed, they will want to complete as much as they can before that happens."

Christopher asked Johnson, "Can you call Amanda Bowers with the CDC? Will she talk to you?"

Jessica informed Johnson, "There isn't much time to fill you in. I would do it as quickly as I could, but I need you to make that call, only if you truly trust her."

* * *

Kevin watched the three of them from his little table in the café. As they headed out, he made a call to let his superior know that he had located Jessica Lathrup and soon none of these three would be a problem.

Their deaths were an unplanned event, but a necessity. By tomorrow morning, the vaccine would be delivered to health clinics across the United States and it would be too late for any of them to stop it.

He watched as they rushed into the hospital. The fools actually believed that they were safe there. He leaned against a flag pole out in front. He flexed his shoulders, rotating them in small circles as he contemplated his next move.

He may as well head back to Dr. Johnson's hotel. The doctor would have to eventually go back there; he would be waiting.

Kevin began to wonder if any of this was truly worth it. There was no doubt that his soul was damned for what he has done, but if these three individuals informed the public of what they were doing, the public would crucify all responsible parties. It would have been smarter to just walk away from the job upon first hearing the plans; however, he feared that just by him knowing the plan was a death sentence for him regardless. There was no way that they would allow any loose strings in their plan.

The results were better than any of them had ever expected. Creating the vaccine with the deadly virus had not been as hard as getting it to just those that were on the list. The unknowing patients in the prisons didn't know what they had agreed to nor did the wardens there.

Once they had verified the virus would not mutate and endanger the lives of others around the inoculated, they had to put the project in motion. Even the testing of the prisoners didn't bother Kevin, because he considered them to be the dregs of humanity; they didn't deserve to live. In fact, their deaths should have been even more painful in his opinion. If he had a say in the matter, the prisoners should be given the same vaccine as the elderly and the ill; that would eliminate a growing cost in this country that was draining our tax dollars.

***

He had been in the hotel lobby for several hours now and wondered just when the doctor would be returning. He had several cups of coffee, read the paper, and observed several very pretty women, who were more than likely having clandestine meetings with hotel guests. More importantly, none of the hotel's security or employees have bothered him. He was dressed in an Armani suit and expensive leather shoes; he blended in with the other business professionals here for a conference. He even had a handcrafted alligator attaché to finish the ensemble.

As he waited for the good doctor to return, his phone rang, "Yes, sir?"

"Do you have any new updates to report?" the man aloofly asked. His dispassionate voice gave Kevin the shivers.

"I have them in my sights."

For a moment, there was nothing but silence. Kevin could actually feel the anger building in the man on the other end of the line. In a low voice he was ordered, "They must be taken care of immediately. We cannot afford to have someone running their mouth, especially to the press."

"Yes, sir."

"Mr. Jameson, you should know that I also do not appreciate that a lowly nobody, some minuscule secretary, was able to decipher our plans. That never should have happened. Do not let it happen again." A moment of silence was experienced before he continued, "Remember, there must be no weapons used. There cannot be a hint of foul play."

As Kevin put away his phone, he took in a deep breath and calmed himself. It should be Randy Erickson's head on a platter and not his. Randy was the one who let the girl get away. He should have known that something was not right as soon as she stayed late that night. Hell, he should have made sure that she couldn't get into Miranda's office in the first place. As of yet, they still had no idea just what it was that she took from the office. They have torn it apart and still had no idea what she could have wanted.

No, there was no way they could let her talk to someone.
They could not take a chance on just what she might know.
A leak would do incredible damage.

These three were easy targets; they were not used to
running from the likes of him. Of course, he has been
wrong before. The accident should have been so simple,
but instead, the good doctor just got up and walked away.

Chapter 50

Johnson was still finding it hard to believe that the U.S. government was responsible for releasing a contaminated vaccine onto the unsuspecting public.

He searched through his phone for Dr. Bowers' number. "Dr. Bowers, this is Dr. Ray Johnson from St. Anne General Hospital in Springport, Louisiana."

"Yes, Dr. Johnson, what is it that I can do for you?"

Taking in a deep breath, he started, "I have something in my possession that I believe you are going to want to see. I have unequivocal evidence that there is a vaccine which attributed to these deaths."

She gasped and quickly said, "But, that can't be. The Food and Drug Administration and even our labs have tested the vaccines. None of the vaccines tested could have caused these deaths."

As he continued on with the story, the words sounded impossible, dramatic and even ridiculous. It belonged in a conspiracy movie and not his current life. "They tested the wrong vaccines. The vaccine responsible for the deaths was not produced by the pharmaceutical companies; it was a vaccine devised by our own government."

Dr. Bowers continued listening and interjecting with questions now and then for clarification, "Wait a minute. Are you saying that these deaths, which are rapidly increasing by the minute, have all been orchestrated by the government? That just doesn't make any sense. Our government wouldn't put all those lives at stake!"

"I'm telling you that this particular vaccine is not safe. I don't have the right equipment here to test it, but I am betting that this vaccine has the deadly strain in it already. I also have paperwork to go with the vaccine."

"Are you saying that I need to warn people that the vaccines are not safe? We have been preaching all along that getting the vaccine is not the cause and the side effects associated with the vaccine are minimal. Oh, but wait, there is one side effect that you should be cautious of, death. We tell these people that the vaccines are the best way to prevent the disease, and now, you are telling me that the prevention is killing them."

Johnson replied, "It is not all the vaccines; it is only the vaccines that are issued to those receiving Medicare and Medicaid, as far as I can tell. You have to see the paperwork to understand just what is happening. It is truly unbelievable."

 "Can you get to Atlanta, Georgia with the information you have?"

Johnson looked at his other two comrades. "I am not sure. We already have someone following us, but we will try. It is an eight hour drive for us, so we need to leave right now."

She informed him, "You should know that seven more states are reporting deaths. People are worried, so the roads will be crazy. It may be best for you to fly here."

"Flying may be too risky. There is too great of a chance that he can get to us from the sky. You should realize that your life may be in danger as well. "

"You may be in the same amount of danger on the road." Johnson thought about it. It was true that someone had already tried to run him off the road once; next time, he may actually be successful.

"Let me see if I can get us plane tickets."

Jessica looked over at Dr. Johnson, "I can't afford a plane ticket. I am almost broke as it is."

Johnson looked at her and explained, "I will pay for your ticket and any expenses that we incur. The most important thing is getting your story to the CDC, so that they can save these people. More deaths have been reported."

Johnson asked Dr. Bowers, "Do you have a death toll as of yet?"

"Reports have confirmed that so far there are well over ten thousand deaths from all over the United States. We now have fifteen states reporting the deadly virus."

"You need to order people to stop going to health clinics for any medical care, including the vaccine. We have to stop people from being inoculated with this deadly vaccine. Tell people that due to the fact that the virus is spreading, it is just too dangerous for anyone to visit clinics at this time. We must ward people off from visiting health clinics, until we can stop this virus."

"I can't do that until I have proof that this vaccine contains the harmful virus." There was a brief moment of silence before she asked, "Do you think Mr. Allen will sit on the story for a little bit longer? You can promise him that he will be allowed interviews and firsthand information, once we figure out just what is going on. I promise that he will be kept in the loop."

Dr. Johnson relayed the question to Christopher. "He said to tell you it is no longer just about the story. He hopes that the information he has will save some lives."

Christopher got Johnson's attention, "I was able to get us plane tickets. We have to go now if we want to catch that plane, though."

Jessica looked at the two men, "What do you think is the safest way to get to the airport?"

Christopher replied, "A taxi is probably the safest, but not a taxi we call."

Johnson shook his head, "No, I know the best way." He walked over to Dr. Adams, "Can I borrow your car for a bit? I have an important meeting that I need to get to."

Adams reached in his pocket for his keys. "I sure hope like hell you are going to a meeting that involves bringing back a cure for this disease."

"I sure hope so."

"Take it for as long as you need it. If you aren't back in time, call me and I will take your shift."

Johnson held out the keys to show Christopher and Jessica that they had a ride, "Let's go."

As they made their way to the airport, a loud beep broke the silence, "This is the Emergency Broadcasting Network. Please stay tuned for an important message from The Department of Health…" An animated voice came across the waves, "The Department of Health would like to encourage everyone to remain calm. As individuals, there are many things you can do to reduce your risk of catching the virus. The first thing is to make sure that you get your vaccine shot. We also encourage keeping your same daily schedule, such as tending to a job, educating children and so forth. Practicing good hygiene is imperative in preventing the spread of germs. It is extremely important that you wash your hands using warm to hot water with antibacterial soap and the use of a hand sanitizer is very important as well. Please remember to use tissues when sneezing, wash your hands after handling tissues and always cover your mouth when coughing. If you do feel sick, you should see your doctor at once; they will give you further instructions on where to go."

Johnson ran his hands through his hair. "Bill Gaudet told me this morning that wellness centers are now set up inside the smaller clinics to help diagnose patients who have the flu. If this is true, it will be harder to keep people away from the very places that are inoculating them with the damn virus."

***

Once inside the plane, Jessica could feel herself finally beginning to relax for a short period of time. She fell asleep almost as soon as the plane left the ground. She did not stir until Christopher woke her up. She woke up hungry, but the short nap seemed to have helped her more than anything.

Now that they were at their destination, she found herself wide awake and extremely nervous. She prayed that this doctor they were going to see could somehow save those who have already received the vaccination. She wished she hadn't been so long in getting the vaccine to someone.

She was surprised at just how silent the conspiracy theorists have remained. Christopher Allen was already starting to put his theory together, so surely others were, too. An unsettling thought suddenly entered her mind. She started to wonder whether the parties responsible for this vaccine and all these deaths were also able to keep the conspiracy theorists from speaking. That very idea suddenly made her extremely uncomfortable. Just how far of a reach did the United States Government have?

Chapter 51

The group of carolers huddled at the corner, stomping their feet and swinging their arms in order to keep warm. Their voices carried through the cold night air before mingling with the harsh sounds of the street traffic. In other areas of the city, Christmas music could be heard blaring from storefront speakers. The Salvation Army Santa's jangled their bells in hopes of last minute donations.

The snow was beginning to fall in a thin sheet. This seasonal display caused traffic to slow down and those walking the streets to shield their eyes from the falling flurries. The snow turned into a slush pile of ice as it hit the ground. Vehicle tires spun on the slick streets and buses were forced to start and stop, to keep from hitting other vehicles.

The black sedan slowly made its way down the icy roads, creeping past the carolers. While the driver was stopped at a light, his passenger rolled down his back window and handed a twenty dollar bill to one of the Santa's. "God Bless you, sir. The Salvation Army appreciates your kindness. Hope you and yours have a Merry Christmas and Happy New Year."

The words fell short to the man in the car, as he rolled his window up, cutting off any further communication. He would not have a Merry Christmas nor would millions of Americans.

As soon as the light turned green, the driver shot forward only to stop short once more. He gripped the steering wheel in place of cursing out loud.

From the back seat, his passenger simply stated, "Take it easy, Staff Sergeant. I would like to get where we are going in one piece."

"Yes sir, General," answered the driver with forced respect for his passenger. There was only one reason the General wanted to go to a seedy motel at this hour of the night; it had nothing to do with his obligation to the United States. What the young man didn't understand was why the General couldn't drive himself? The worst thing about this assignment was being forced to drive a small sedan, instead of one of the larger SUV's that were made to drive in this kind of weather. If they did get the snowfall that was forecasted, the little sedan would be struggling to make it back to Fort Detrick, Maryland.

This was definitely not how he had anticipated spending his duty shift tonight. Unfortunately, this was not the first time the Staff Sergeant had made this type of trip in the last six months, but lately, they seem to be more frequent. This woman must be something special for him to want to step out at this late hour in these weather conditions; however, the Staff Sergeant knew his place and would not say anything. If he wanted to make rank, it was best to take orders and play along with whatever the General ordered.

As the motel came into sight, Thompson took out the vial and poured its contents into the bottle of scotch. There was enough of the virus in the scotch to kill the intended victim quickly. Upon autopsy, it would look as if Daniel

Wright succumbed to the same virus as so many others have here in the United States. Daniel has kept himself isolated these last few days, so this made it easier for them to honestly say they didn't even know he was sick. He has given them the perfect opportunity without even realizing it.

****

Daniel Wright looked at his watch. He wondered why a meeting had been called at this hour. All he wanted to do was curl up in bed and fall sound asleep, but he knew that if he didn't show there would be questions; questions that he was not ready to answer. As he made his way to the hotel, he looked around as he had for years. When working with ruthless people, you tended to always watch your back.

Before walking into the room, he tried to organize his thoughts. He wouldn't allow Kevin or Gregory to distract him tonight. Adrenaline fed his over developed paranoia, as he feared that his life would soon come to an end. Should he hint that if something were to ever happen to him that he had a backup plan? No, that could put his best friend's life in grave danger. It was best to leave things be. A smirk formed on his face. The fools have underestimated him.

He wished he had the courage to send the documents prior to his death, but he never found it. He knew in his heart of hearts that the American public needed to know what they have done, but he was unable to bear them looking at him in disgust. No, he has spent too many years creating a reputation and with one simple order, it had all gone up in smoke. He truly wished he had the courage to admit his part in this while alive, but at least his death would be avenged.

Daniel opened the hotel room to find the other men there, except for the President. Thompson handed Daniel a drink. "Gentlemen, thanks for coming on such short notice. I thought it was time that Kevin caught us up on all that was happening."

Daniel took a long hard swallow of his drink, walked over to the bar and poured himself another drink. He could hardly wait for this meeting to begin. As he listened to Kevin's report, he found it getting hot in the room. He adjusted his tie as he tried to concentrate on what Jameson was staying.

Suddenly, he stood up, "Gentlemen, I am sorry to interrupt the meeting, but I am not feeling well. If you don't mind, I believe I will go home."

Thompson looked over at Daniel. "You don't look very well, my friend. Would you like my driver to take you home?"

Shaking his head, he answered, "No, I will be fine. It is probably just my allergies acting up."

As Daniel headed home, he could feel himself getting worse. How ironic was it that he felt as bad as he did. Could it be that karma was reaching out to him?

It took him a good hour to get back home. Not only was the distance a problem, but with him feeling as bad as he did, had it become hard to keep the road in focus.

His home was in a well gated, exclusive neighborhood. There were only a dozen or so houses here, all owned by lawyers, politicians, CEOs, and surgeons. He had winced at the price tag, but his ex-wife convinced him that if you wanted the best you had to pay for it and that he did.

His father was probably rolling in his grave at the extravagant life Daniel currently lived. His father had been a penny pincher to the ninth degree. They all had to wear their shoes until there had been gaping holes and the soles would fall off. He didn't care if shoes fit; they just had to wear what they had. His mother would mend socks, repair zippers, and replace buttons, rather than buying new things. They never were allowed to splurge on anything. Buying anything new had been out of necessity, not want.

Despite the penny pinching and heavy hand, Daniel indeed learned a lot from his dad. He learned the importance of tucking a little money aside for a rainy day; that certainly had been a blessing when the stock markets fell. He did not lose his shirt as others had.

The oversized mahogany door opened before he could reach it and a small, Mexican woman looked at him. "Sir, I wasn't expecting you home so soon. Are you okay?" she asked with fluent English. Maria's family had moved to America long before her birth, and she was raised up north, so there wasn't much of an accent in her speech.

His shoes snapped loudly against the imported Italian marble tiles of the entry way, as he made his way into the house, "I do feel a little under the weather, Maria. I plan on going straight to bed. Maybe all I need is a little rest."

Before heading to his room, Daniel stepped into his office. He shrugged out of his suit coat, laid it across an oversized leather chair and moved to the bar for a quick drink.

He rolled his neck, as he released some of the tension that hung over him while at the meeting. Reaching across the granite top of the bar, he poured a glass of whiskey. He had finally acquired a taste for scotch, but he still preferred his twenty year old whiskey better.

His house was small, compared to others in the neighborhood, but he still saw it as an enormous monstrosity. His ex-wife picked out the house right after their marriage. He considered it a waste of money, but after she left him for her tennis coach, he kept it just for spite. She had fought tooth and nail for the house, as well as half of his money. She would have been better off filing for divorce in another state. The stupid woman never thought for once that a judge would hold her to the prenuptial agreement; besides, he had her on infidelity, as well as knowing most of the judges here.

There were still parts of the house that bore marks of Sylvia's hands; after all, she did have an eye for design, but even while married, he refused to allow her to decorate his office. It was opulent, but masculine. There were heavy, rich brown leather couches and chairs, butter soft. There was the granite bar, antique lawyer's desk and other fine pieces of furniture in the room. No, he certainly could not let her touch his office; it was his place.

He took another sip of whiskey and grimaced as the amber liquid burned on the way down. His throat was getting worse and there was a definite chill to the air.

Chapter 52

Thompson walked in the room. "The job is done."

He continued looking at the computer screen in front of him, before slowly turning around. The steel blue eyes under gray eyebrows seemed to pierce right through him. A shiver snaked across his back at the intense stare. He felt as if he was a butterfly pinned to a board.

He walked over to the humidor and took out two cigars. Just from looking at the man's hands, you could tell he has never done a true hard day's work in recent years. His nails were perfectly manicured and there were no callouses to be found.

In one fluid movement, he took out his silver lighter and lit both cigars, before handing one to Thompson. They each took a long puff of the cigar. Their mouths turned up in pleasure, as the complex flavors teased their palates and the medium bodied smoke was inhaled.

As they continued to smoke their cigars in silence, Thompson could still feel the man's eyes boring right into his skull. For a moment, he felt like a puppet on a string. He pushed his shoulders back, straightening his form. Weakness in any form was not a trait he cared to display and one that was not tolerated by the man in front of him.

"That is one problem solved then, excellent work. It appears, though, that we may have another problem. My sources are telling me that the CDC doctor is refusing to stop her investigation. She visited a local Atlanta hospital, where she obtained several blood samples."

Thompson nodded his head, as he was unworried about her investigating the matter. "Let her investigate. There is no way that the flu virus can be tracked back down to the vaccine. If need be, we can slip a few of the vaccines to surrounding facilities."

Stroking his chin, he contemplated what he was being told. "Hmm, that could work. It would throw her off the trail of it simply being the vaccines offered for free. I like the way you think. It would be more or less playing Russian Roulette with the lives of those we never intended to kill."

"As you once told me, there are always casualties in war."

Kingsley took another deep puff of his cigar. "I understand we also have a reporter who is pursuing this story as well."

"Kevin is on his trail."

"Kevin is turning out to be useless. He let the doctor get away from him and I don't hold much belief in him being able to dispose of the reporter as well."

Thompson nodded his head in agreement, "He is getting rather messy."

"I would like these matters resolved quickly, but it has to look like an accident."

"You do not have to worry; the deaths will look like Daniel's. It would be easy to have a spiked drink served to them."

The man's voice dropped down low, barely audible for a moment. "It will be nothing that can be traced back to us, correct?"

Thompson nodded his head in acknowledgement. "That is the beauty of this. It is a highly concentrated virus that acts quicker than the one housed in the vaccine."

"Brilliant. It appears that your education has served you well."

"So, do we know where the reporter and good doctors are presently, or is Kevin still searching for them?"

"He assured me he has them cornered."

The man sighed, almost imperceptibly. "Be sure that he completes his task." With that comment, he left, slipping out like a ghost.

***

Clifford Wellington mourned for his friend's death in silence. He and Daniel Wright have been the closest of friends since elementary school; when Daniel came to him with the requests, he didn't think twice about it; however, when Daniel mentioned that it was imperative that he made sure the packages couldn't be traced back to Clifford, he began to worry about what he had gotten himself into.

Clifford thought back to the night before Daniel had passed away. Daniel didn't sound sick in the slightest; he did sound stressed out. He heard the rumors on television about the virus acting quickly when one has contracted it, but death in

only a few hours? That just didn't seem possible, especially
with a man as healthy as Daniel

Upon Daniel's death, Clifford messengered the first package
to Dr. Bowers with the CDC. As per Daniel's instructions,
the other remaining packages were to be mailed tomorrow
morning.

Chapter 53

As Johnson, Christopher, and Jessica disembarked from the plane, they caught the news broadcast. Jessica looked over at Christopher, "I have seen his name on several memos floating around the office."

Christopher ran his hand through his hair, "This is getting serious. If they are murdering at the cabinet level, our lives are in serious trouble."

"If the government could order the deaths of millions of elderly, what makes you think they would stop at murdering one of their own? Besides, most of these men are probably military and have been trained to kill."

Johnson reminded them, "But when the Secretary of Defense is killed, someone has to feel threatened."

Christopher stated, "If the Secretary of Defense knew about this, who else knows about it? We know about the President, but there has to be more key players involved in this. It would take a group of people to perform a task this monumental."

Johnson nodded his head in agreement. "And if they are killing off their own men, then there must be dissension in the ranks."

Jessica added, "I have a very uncomfortable feeling about all of this. Someone is playing some serious hard ball here."

Christopher replied, "I believe that someone is beginning to get scared, and when people get scared, they tend to be very unreliable."

"Yes, but what exactly are they afraid of? Is it just that they were afraid Daniel Wright was going to blow the whistle on them or is it something much worse?"

As the three entered the building which housed the Center for Disease Control, a messenger pulled up to the front door and parked. He carried the package immediately to the front desk as instructed and asked for Dr. Amanda Bowers.

Chapter 54

The President waited patiently for a status report. So far, he was pleased with the results. They have been able to keep everything contained just as he hoped.

Thompson materialized in front of him. Without speaking, Thompson walked over to the bar and poured each of them a drink. Ice rattled softly in the tumblers, as he sat down the glass in front of the President. The silence hung heavy in the room. The clink of the ice seemed loud and out of place.

The president raised the glass to his lips and took a long swallow of the amber liquid before he set the glass back down. Thompson took a sip of his scotch before speaking. "Sir, I just wanted to let you know that all systems are still a "go".

He nodded his head, "Perfect. What about Kevin?"

"He said that all on his end is taken care of. He has yet to elaborate further, but you do not have to worry; I am keeping very close tabs on him."

Tapping his index fingers together, he looked directly at Thompson. The man sitting in front of him was in no way a novice. He was perfect for the position he was in. Not only was he very careful, but he was just as powerful and dangerous. "This is a dangerous game that we have begun. Now that everything is in place, I do not want anything to stop this plan."

"You have nothing to worry about, sir; the protocol will not be broken. There are too many wheels turning now for it to be stopped. The plan has begun and the backfield is in motion. Now, all we have to do is sit and wait for the results."

The President conceded, "I must say that I am pleased thus far. Even if this doesn't work to the full extent that I had hoped, we will see some success to varying degrees." As he stared directly into the Thompson's eyes, he added, "You must also understand that I want to make sure that we do not have to worry about any leaks."

Thompson nodded his understanding. "I do understand, sir. No one would want to find out that their President was capable of such orders."

"I will not be the only one who goes down, remember that. The citizens of the United States will also wonder why no one tried to stop me." Sighing, he added, "No one will understand that the state of the governmental affairs is in such disarray that this was the only way to handle the situation. They will view me as a treasonous President, but no one has ever done anything so extraordinary to save this country."

"No, sir, it is best that no one knows just what took place."

The President of the United States informed Thompson, "I believe what we are doing is the right course for this country. I do not want anyone attempting to stop us."

Chapter 55

Kevin stood by the car rental kiosk and casually scanned the crowds. If his intel was correct, the good doctor and his two companions should be disembarking from the plane right about now.

He has patiently waited here for two hours, just in case they had somehow managed to catch an earlier flight. His safest and best bet would be to somehow inject all three of them with the vaccine while they waited for their luggage. Each vaccine along with its needle was carefully concealed in a ring he had on each hand. The only problem was that would just take care of two problems. The third vaccine he had to be a little more deceptive with. The vaccine gun was tucked away in his pants' pocket. For now, his current plan was to accidentally bump into the other person and inject them. To do this, he would have to act as if he was drunk. He would simply stumble into the first person; grab a shoulder of the other two while pretending to hold himself upright. By the time they realized that they have indeed been injected, he would be long gone.

Up until now, they have been incredibly lucky in escaping, but their luck was about to change. He heard the arrival announcement of their plane as it came across the PA system. A few passengers were already beginning to stand at the luggage carousel. As he caught sight of them walking from the gate to baggage claim, he made sure that everything was ready.

He let out a curse under his breath as the trio completely bypassed the carousel. After they were a few feet from him, he began to follow. Kevin made sure to climb into the taxi right behind them. "I need you to follow that taxi," he instructed the driver.

"It'll cost you extra."

"If you lose sight of them it will cost you dearly, you understand me?"

He simply nodded his head and followed the cab in front of him. With Atlanta traffic being as busy as it was, Kevin was impressed that his taxi cab driver could keep them in his sights as well as he did. Half an hour after their arrival in Atlanta, they pulled up to the CDC building.

Kevin slammed his fist hard against the back of the taxi cab driver's seat. There was no way that he could follow them into the CDC, and if they were here, that could only mean one thing for all of them, TROUBLE! Paying the driver, he exited the car and decided to wait for them to exit the building. Before he could kill them, though, he would need to find out just what they have told the CDC.

Chapter 56

Connie Farmington could not believe their luck. She has been volunteering here at St. Vincent De Paul Shelter for almost three years and in all that time, this was the first time the United States Government had surprised her by bringing in a mobile health clinic to give free flu shots to the homeless who frequented their shelter. All she could do was thank God for their generosity.

Word must have spread quickly through the streets, because by lunch time, the shelter was full of homeless waiting for their flu shot. They all knew that living on the streets was hard, but come flu season, it was almost a guarantee that they would succumb to the disease. Maybe, thanks to the government, this would prevent some of them from getting so sick.

***

Earl Humphrey walked at a slow, unsteady pace along the uneven sidewalk. His face was the color of pasty chalk. He had to stop more and more often to cough. He has felt bad ever since last night or maybe it was closer to lunchtime. All he knew for certain was that his lungs were on fire, his head felt as if a bomb went off inside of it and his body was burning up. Even with the wind chill at twenty degrees, he had broken out in a cold sweat.

This was the first time in a very long time that he wished he had a bed to curl up in. He tried to push his way through the crowd of people in Times Square. All he wanted to do was get to the alley he has called home these last few months, pull the blanket he found the other day over his head, and fall sound asleep. As tired as he was, the street noise wouldn't even be able to keep him up.

A horn from an impatient driver sounded behind him, causing him to jump. The lights, the noise and the filth of the city seemed to surround him, as another violent coughing attack wracked through his body. He thought this time the cough may never end, as it kept going on and on. He doubled over, as the coughing fit grew worse. On the sidewalk, people began to walk around him; making sure to stay a far distance away.

He fell to the ground, landing on his hands and knees. He was too weak to stand up; instead, he rolled onto his side, as a stabbing pain moved through his body. He tried to move into a sitting position, but with every little movement he feared he would black out.

The people on the street walked past him and not a single person even bothered to look down at him. He should not be surprised, though. New Yorkers have learned to completely ignore the homeless that lived on the streets here.

With more and more people joining the masses of the homeless that littered the streets of New York, the people living here have become increasingly insensitive. As Earl breathed his last breath, not one person even noticed.

***

Two blocks over from Earl was another homeless man who always knew that one day he would die on the mean streets of New York City. He figured he would be stabbed to death, but instead, he rolled over in his cardboard box and took his last breath.

As the homeless bodies began to crowd the coroner's office, more pine boxes were ordered for their burial. The coroner's office was already overworked and underpaid, so they did not even bother with a simple autopsy. The bodies of the homeless victims were quickly sent off to their numbered graves. If the bodies were left in the streets or burial was delayed, then there was too great of a chance for secondary diseases to spread rapidly.

Chapter 57

By five o'clock that afternoon, Wayne Sinclair couldn't wait to get home. At the age of sixty-five, he honestly thought he would be retired and playing golf all day, but instead, they lost all of their retirement savings, forcing him to work for a few more years.

He never even noticed how erratically he was driving his Grand Jeep Cherokee on the way home. At the stoplight, he took out his handkerchief to mop the sweat streaming down his face. He seemed to be turning paler by the minute and his skin was cold and clammy. As he got closer to home, his body was suddenly attacked with a harsh coughing fit.

He continued driving erratically as he pulled into the tree lined street of his subdivision. Parking his car cockeyed in his driveway, he stumbled inside. Normally, he brought his work home, but with this being a Friday night, all he wanted to do was relax and not think about it.

His wife, Sheila, called out from upstairs, "I'll be down in a minute. Why don't you fix us a drink before we head to Angela and David's house?" Their son and daughter-in-law just had their first child, their first grandchild, and Angela wanted to have all the grandparents over for supper tonight. Of course, coming to see the baby was another reason for the visit as well. Wayne wasn't sure who was more proud of the new baby, the grandparents or the actual parents.

Wayne felt too tired to even walk in the house, so he shuffled his body into the living room and plopped down on the couch. Sheila came bouncing down the stairs, her normal energetic and bubbly self. She stopped and stared at her husband, as she took in his pale face, "Oh, honey you look like you feel awful. Should I call the kids and tell them we can't make it tonight?"

Shaking his head, he said, "No, I will be fine; besides, you have been looking forward to this all week."

Sheila bent down and kissed her husband on the forehead. "I need to go get the thermometer. You are burning up."

Wayne grabbed her hand before she left. "No. I promise I will be fine. Why don't you fix us a drink and just let me rest for a bit."

Wayne could hear the ice hitting the glass and forced himself to sit up. He loosened his tie and eased his jacket off, just letting it drop behind him on the couch. His recliner was only a few short feet from where he was currently sitting, but right now, it seemed miles away.

***

Sheila watched her husband from the corner of her eye. She has never seen him look as sick as he did right now. She knew that he has been pushing himself hard at work to show that he could keep up with the younger salesmen, but maybe it was time for him to retire. They could learn to live on less income. It was better than him having another heart attack. Five years ago, she thought they had lost him for good.

At least the weekend was here and he could rest. She knew
there was no way she would have gotten him to call in sick
tomorrow. He never took sick days or even vacation,
because he feared that the younger salesmen would step in
and steal his current customers. With the economy the way
it was, everyone was watching their spending and it was
harder to make new clients.

***

As Wayne took the glass of whiskey and coke from her, he
found it extremely hard to just keep his eyes open. He
rubbed the back of his neck as another coughing attack hit
him. He reached into his pocket and pulled out his
handkerchief to wipe down his brow once more.

Sheila looked over at her husband with concern clearly
evident on her face. He smiled over at her weakly, "I am
fine. It was just a hectic day at work." Sighing deeply, he
said, "It may be time for me to admit that my age is finally
catching up to me."

He took a drink of his cocktail and let the amber liquid
soothe its way down his throat. "I'll be fine in no time at
all."

"Can I get you something, possibly an aspirin?"

Shaking his head, he replied, "I promise you, I am fine. It's
nothing."

She reached over and squeezed his hand. She was worried
about just how hot his skin was to the touch. "Are you sure
it isn't your heart? I can call the doctor and see if he can
see you. There is also the flu going around."

Annoyed at the mothering his wife was giving him, he snipped, "I am fine, Sheila."

Wayne slumped back on the couch, rubbing his eyelids before taking another swallow of his now diluted drink. Before he could swallow the drink, he was hit by another deep, hacking cough that wrenched his insides.

His mind told him that his wife was right and he needed to go to the doctor, but he feared that he would be admitted to the hospital. After his heart attack, hospitals made him nervous. He hated not being the one in control, and there also was the fact that he would be surrounded by all the sick and dying.

Unable to convince Wayne that they should stay home, they headed out to their son's house with Sheila driving. Once there, Sheila helped Wayne up the drive and into the house. David helped his dad into the recliner, "Dad, are you sure you feel okay?"

"I am fine. Your mother just misses having you around to nurture, so she thought she needed to be my nurse."

Sheila walked over with the baby, "Okay, okay. I will leave you alone." Kissing her grandson, she added, "Besides, I can love up on this little guy."

Before she came any closer to him, he held up his hand while shaking his head. "I can see him from here." Covering his mouth when he was attacked with another round of coughs. "I don't want to get the baby sick."

The others in the room looked at each other in surprise; they thought he would want to see the grandchild. He smiled over at them, trying to hide how ill he really was. David noticed his dad's pale face and began to worry. He was really sick. "Dad, I think I should take you to the emergency room."

"No, no. I just need to get home and go to bed. I am just overly tired is all; besides, I just had the flu shot yesterday."

David looked at his dad. "Dad, I don't think this is just a little cold that you are dealing with. I really think you should go see a doctor."

Right now, all he wanted to do was sleep. "No, I don't want any more doctors!"

As another coughing fit hit him, he dropped to the floor in pain. It seemed as if his lungs were going to burst at any moment. The cough was so severe that he ended up vomiting right there. With David's help, Sheila got her husband to the car.

On the short drive home, Sheila kept a close eye on him. He didn't look good at all. His color seemed to be getting worse and his eyes were hollow. As if reading her thoughts, "I just need some rest. Everything will be fine."

Chapter 58

Dr. Ryan Young was exhausted. He looked at the patient's chart that the nurse had handed him. The elderly man lying on the exam table looked much older than sixty-five. The oxygen mask hid much of his lower face, but it was needed, as his breathing became labored.

The nurse informed Dr. Young, "The wife said that he started showing flu symptoms yesterday afternoon. She called the paramedics this morning when his symptoms began to worsen."

Above the gurney, the IV bag dripped clear fluid back into his body. As Dr. Young began his physical exam, the nurse placed him on a cardiac monitor, which bleated with each irregular heartbeat. "Mr. Sinclair, I see that you suffered a mild myocardial infarction several years ago. I just want you to know that your heart is good. That irregular heartbeat you hear on the monitor is considered normal for you."

After listening to the man's short rapid breaths, Dr. Young asked, "So, Mr. Sinclair, your wife mentioned that you started feeling bad yesterday afternoon. Is that correct?"

William Sinclair had difficulty responding. He couldn't seem to find his voice and he was even weaker than when he woke up this morning. "Yesterday at work… Nurse… warned… I wouldn't… feel… good… after… shot."

"Mr. Sinclair, this is very important. What shot did you receive?"

Sheila answered for him, "He went and got his flu shot yesterday morning. I was supposed to go with him, but when we got to the clinic, it was only for those on Medicare. I have another five years before I am on it, so I just went to my doctor's office to get the vaccine."

Outside the exam room, Dr. Young told the nurse, "I want blood gases, hematocrit, urine, and a complete work up. Also, we need to move him out of the emergency room and put him with the other flu patients."

Taking a deep breath, he pulled out Dr. Bowers' card and dialed her number, "Dr. Bowers, this is Dr. Ryan Young. We have several more patients admitted since you were last here. I just admitted a patient receiving his flu vaccine yesterday and his wife also had the flu vaccine yesterday morning. He is extremely ill and she is showing no signs of the flu. I just wanted to let you know, as we thought the common denominator with all these patients was the flu vaccine, and with this new information, we need to look elsewhere for the connection."

Dr. Bowers asked, "This is very important. Did she say if she received the flu vaccine at the same place?"

"No, she did not. She said something about not having Medicare yet, so she had to go to her doctor's office."

***

Upon her arrival at the hospital, Amanda's stomach was filled with dread. There was a TV truck with its antennae extended sitting at the front entrance. She would have to change her direction so that she was not spotted walking into the hospital. The last thing she wanted was to be bombarded by a bunch of news reporters.

Dr. Young saw Dr. Bowers come through the ER, "What's going on? Are the patients in the isolation room?"

"I take it you haven't seen the front of the hospital?"

"I've been a little busy here."

Amanda sighed, "It appears that the news of the virus and deaths have reached the media. The front is crawling with TV trucks and news reporters."

As soon as the elevator doors opened to the recently transformed ICU ward, the meaning of his statement hit her full force. They have been extremely busy here. There were at least thirty patients on this floor.

In each of the rooms was a nurse tending to patients. There were members of the medical staff adjusting blankets, offering water and smoothing hair out of the faces. Medical carts lined the halls with pitchers of ice, towels, blankets and even body bags. Dr. Young explained, "We can no longer keep the rooms private with only one patient to a room. We are able to fit four cots in each room. If this keeps up, though, we will have to look at another place to keep the ill."

"Are these the same patients admitted earlier?"

Grimly he stated, "Unfortunately, no. The number of patients is increasing rapidly. The surrounding hospitals are also seeing an increase in numbers."

Picking up her phone, she called her secretary, "Can you please get me an estimate on the number of people who are on Medicaid and Medicare here in Atlanta? Afterwards, please see if you can get me numbers for other areas as well?"

"I will get right on it."

Amanda looked over at Dr. Young, "I think we need an accurate number of patients that we may be dealing with."

"What about asking everyone not to have the vaccination at this time?"

"Right now, I do not have any solid proof that the vaccination is the direct cause of the virus. If I am wrong and make the announcement, the pharmaceutical companies will hang me out to dry."

"But, wouldn't it be better to be safe and worry about the consequences later?"

She shook her head, "I have a feeling I am already overstepping my boundaries. I have already caught a lot of flak from my supervisors."

"It seems that they would want to resolve this as well."

"That's what I thought, too, but it seems that they feel as if this is simply a highly volatile virus season. They keep saying they warned everyone it would be a bad season."

Dr. Young ran his hand through his hair. "I understand that we will always have a few deaths with each flu season, especially with the elderly and patients with a compromised immune system, but this…"

"I agree, but my hands are pretty much tied. The powers that be do not see it the same as we do. They see the patients as only the elderly and those with an already compromised immune system as the ones dying." She let out a deep sigh, "I have a feeling if it was healthy men and women dying then we would be looking at a completely different scenario."

Dr. Bowers looked the young doctor directly in the eyes, "You need to be extremely careful who you talk to with regards to your beliefs. This is proving to be very dangerous for anyone who comes close to the truth."

Swallowing hard, he nodded his head, "I understand."

"If you would prefer, I can assign you to the CDC, where you can help us research the samples we have collected."

"No, I can't leave these people. As crazy as this may sound, I do feel as if I have possibly helped these patients somewhat. I know that I am unable to heal them, but I do feel as if maybe I am helping them find some relief before they move to the next realm. Some of these people have no loved ones to hold their hands as they die. No one should die alone."

* * *

 As soon as Amanda returned to her office, she started receiving alerts from other U.S. cities notifying the CDC that a fatal strain of influenza had indeed hit their city. The cities now reporting alerts included San Antonio, Dallas, Fort

Worth, New Orleans, Los Angeles, Miami, Seattle, Des Moines, and Branson. There were more hospitals than Amanda could even fathom reporting cases. The only thing they could ascertain for certain was that this particular strain seemed to be very selective with whom it killed.

Right now, she was extremely grateful that this virus was not contagious. If this virus would be contagious, she feared it could possibly wipe out almost all of humanity. She prayed that it did not mutate and evolve into a contagious virus. If it became contagious and there was no cure found, there was no doubt in her mind that these would be humanities last days on earth.

She kept telling herself that it was only showing up in the most vulnerable of the population. That told her that this virus attacked by vulnerability and not contagion; besides, if it was contagious, they would be seeing many more patients presenting with the virus. The incubation period of this particular virus was too short to say otherwise.

Chapter 59

Jane, Dr. Bowers' secretary, signed for the package while she looked at the three visitors. "And you say that Dr. Bowers is expecting you?"

Dr. Johnson nodded his head, "She is."

"Well, she was called to the general hospital here, but should be back soon."

Christopher looked directly into the secretary's eye. "It is imperative that we talk to Dr. Bowers right away. It has to do with what may be causing the deadly virus."

Jane had a gut feeling that whatever this man was talking about was highly important. "Let me call her right now."

"Dr. Bowers, I know you are busy, but there are three people waiting to see you."

Amanda let out a tired sigh, "Who is it?"

"A Dr. Johnson and two others are standing in front of me saying that you are expecting them."

Upon hearing that the three have indeed made it to Atlanta, Amanda found a renewed energy inside of her. "Tell them I will be there as soon as I can."

"One more thing, you just had a package delivered to you that stated "Extremely Important"."

"Does it say from whom?"

"There is no label and no return address, but it already went through security and has passed inspection."

Dr. Bowers gave her secretary further instructions, "Please show Dr. Johnson and his guests to my office. Afterwards, do you think you can check out what is inside the package?"

"Yes, ma'am."

***

As soon as Jane arrived back at her desk, she carefully opened the package. Seeing who the opening letter was from, she let out a surprised gasp. Inside of the package was a rather large packet of papers, a flash drive, and a small canister similar to what they used here to hold blood samples in.

She immediately called Dr. Bowers. "Dr. Bowers, I think you may want to come back into the office as soon as possible. That package delivered here for you has very important documents and samples related to the virus you are fighting."

Dr. Bowers looked at all the patients and hated to leave. "Who is it from?"

"Daniel Wright."

There was a moment of silence, while Dr. Bowers thought about what Jane just said. She tried to place that name, "Daniel Wright? Isn't he the Secretary of Defense?"

"Yes. Wasn't his death blamed on the virus?"

Dr. Bowers let out a long whistle, "Damn. Jane, do NOT tell anyone else about the package. I'm not even sure if it is safe for us to talk about this over the phone."

Chapter 60

Dr. Amanda Bowers, Dr. Johnson, Christopher, and Jessica all sat around the desk in stunned silence. Her desk was littered with documents.

The room was silent as they stared at the information in front of them. The past hour has been a haze, as they reviewed the information. Now, it was time for Dr. Bowers to decide which way to go from here. She had all the documentation she needed to prove the vaccine had been manufactured by the United States Government to end millions of lives.

Christopher has already started writing the story in his head. "Incriminating documents were secured by a staff reporter, indicating that the United States Government is responsible for the deaths of United States citizens through a specially formulated vaccine. All of this was done to reportedly save the U.S. Government money and help to decrease the deficit. The Center for Disease Control is now working around the clock and is intent on finding a cure for the virus that has infected American citizens. In the meantime, this deadly virus will continue to kill at an exponentially fast rate."

He couldn't wait to get back to his hotel room and continue working on the article. It needed a little more finessing, but he had the outline completed. If he wasn't here with all these professionals, he would jump up and let out a loud whoop. His mouth curved upwards, as a slow smile formed.

Out of nowhere, Dr. Johnson screamed out, "I will be damned! We were so busy reviewing the documents that we did not even bother to open the canister yet."

Dr. Bowers stated, "I figured it had another sample of the vaccine that Jessica already provided us."

"It does, but it also has the cure."

"Those sons of bitches had a cure this whole time! They let all of these innocent men and women die, and some were children. What makes this worse is this was orchestrated so they could save some money."

Christopher looked at the two doctors. "Do you think that the CDC will be able to recreate the cure?"

"I am going to get it over to the lab right now. I also plan on having my boss contact the necessary officials. Something tells me that they have more than one cure already made. If not, they would have already noticed that there was a sample missing."

With sadness in her voice, Jessica stated, "I never saw anything about a cure in Miranda's office. If I had, I would have taken that as well."

Christopher looked over at her, "They more than likely never told Miranda a cure was available."

Chapter 61

Kevin slowly made the phone call, as he swallowed down the lump that had grown in his throat, "They know. It won't be long before it is all over the press. It is time for some decisive action, Mr. President."

Kevin waited for a reply. Currently, they were rats trapped in a maze. "Right now, let's wait and see what move they make."

"Mr. President, I don't think that is the wisest plan."

"You heard me! I don't want to make any moves until we know just what we are up against. You have her office bugged correct?"

"Yes, sir."

The President ordered, "Well then, do what you were told to do. Listen in and find out just what the hell they know."

Kevin set up his equipment and began to listen in on the conversations taking place. This was a disaster and it was just going to get worse. To top it off, shit always rolled downhill, which meant that his head would be on the chopping block for this. He has warned and advised the President just what should have been done and now it was too late.

Well, he did know one way that may save his skin and he planned on doing just that. As he listened to the chatter in the room, he started his car and headed towards the office of the Federal Bureau of Investigation. He planned on turning state's evidence in an attempt to save part of his sorry hide.

Mindlessly, he took a swig of water and winced, as the stale water hit his throat. As he turned into the FBI building, he could feel the beginnings of a sore throat. *Son of a bitch!* They have somehow gotten to him. Well, little did they know, but it had screwed them as well. There may be no fingerprints on the bottle, but there would be traces of the flu pathogen in the water. Taking his briefcase, the water bottle and everything else, he walked into the building. At the guard's desk, he simply placed a gun on the desk. In a matter of seconds, he was being escorted into an interrogation room.

***

Thompson walked calmly towards the entrance. In his right hand was a metal briefcase like those that he has seen other CDC doctor's carrying inside the building.

Once he made it past security, he walked over to the receptionist, "I am with the Department of Health. I was hoping to see Dr. Bowers regarding the current influenza outbreak." He pulled his identification from his jacket pocket to show her.

Bethany felt instant disdain for this man. There was something antagonistic about him that rubbed her the wrong way. His body language read authoritarian. "I'm sorry, but Dr. Bowers is in a meeting right now."

"I am trying to liaise with the CDC with regards to the influenza outbreak. Time is of the essence."

The receptionist offered, "I can call Dr. Bowers' secretary and let her know you are down here."

"If you would just point me in the right direction, I can let her know myself. Maybe by the time I get up there, Dr. Bowers will be free."

"Her office is on the fourth floor, fifth office to the right." The more she listened to this man talk, there was no denying that he was military or had a military background. He could claim all he wanted that he was from the Department of Health, but she knew that was a lie.

As soon as he was in the elevator, she picked up the phone. "I believe the man you are on the lookout for is on his way up."

After the call was made, alerts were made to the agents. Since the CDC building was a complicated area to secure, they had to also use members of the local police force as well.

As the lights over the elevator door indicated which floor the elevator had reached, the agents prepared to respond. When the doors opened, Thompson was surprised to find that the corridor was practically empty. He figured with all that was going on, people would be busy. Maybe Kevin was wrong in his assumption that Dr. Bowers went to the press.

He made his way to Dr. Bowers' office with slow and deliberate movements. To the casual observer, he looked like someone heading to a meeting. Nothing he did looked in any way suspicious. Little did anyone know that inside the briefcase was a bomb that would begin its countdown once set down.

All Thompson planned on doing was handing Dr. Bowers' secretary a business card and leaving the briefcase near her desk. He would have exactly five minutes to leave the building before the bomb detonated. When it did, it would take out a good portion of the building, including Dr. Bowers' office and any evidence that she had in her possession.

Just as he was moving in, he heard a voice from behind. "Put your hands up slowly."

The FBI agent moved in from behind, carefully removing the briefcase from his hands and handed it over to the bomb squad agent standing by. No one could possibly know what he had planned, but they wanted to be prepared for anything and everything. No sooner than he passed through the security checkpoint, the hidden cameras picked up the outline of the bomb hidden inside the briefcase.

Epilogue

"This is Steven Luxby with Channel Ten News. The virus that swept the nation is now nothing more than a painful memory. Officials with the United States Center for Disease Control and Department of Health are officially telling everyone that the virus has been contained and the worry is over. They do want to remind everyone that preventive measures are still important with any illness, especially with the elderly and high-risk. They do understand the public's reluctance to receive a vaccine, but it is highly recommended that you put your trust in the pharmaceutical companies to look out for your best interests.

"The President of the United States as well as other members who played key roles in this deadly vaccine are currently being held at a secret location until their hearings. A total of seven hundred thousand people have died so far from the contaminated vaccines. The numbers from this deadly vaccine have outnumbered the deaths as a result of the 1918 influenza outbreak, in which six hundred seventy five thousand people lost their lives.

"Thanks to the CDC, a cure has been given to the remaining patients receiving the contaminated vaccine. It is truly a shame that the cure was not discovered before the lives of so many were claimed. Although the virus lasted only a few short weeks, its effects will last a lifetime for those involved."

The camera panned in for a close up of the reporter. With a smile he added, "If it hadn't been for a diligent reporter, a zealous doctor, and a determined doctor with the CDC, there is a chance that the mystery surrounding the sudden rash of fatalities in the elderly and other high risk patients may never have been discovered. The Unites States Government has once again been rocked by a presidential scandal. The FBI is also looking into a few other suspicious deaths that may be associated with the scandal as well. We will keep you apprised of future developments as they arise."

What had started out as a way to end the deficit has bankrupted the U.S. Government. The families of all the victims have filed suit. All parties involved are being prosecuted to the fullest extent of the law. No bail would be set for any member involved in this plan; each person involved is being considered just as dangerous as those involved in the Nazi war camps.

Bill Kingsley turned off the television set, not wanting to hear anymore. A smile formed on his lips, as he thought of how all the king's men came falling down; that was all except for the king. All of his moves had been in secret. No one knew of his existence; except one and he was no longer able to talk. There was no one left to identify him as the mastermind. He looked over the list of Senators and Congressmen wondering which one to befriend next. There was still much to be done.

Thank you!

Dear Reader,

Thank you for purchasing this book. I hope you enjoyed reading this novel as much as I enjoyed writing it.

It is very important for me to hear what you think about the book. Your reviews give me inspiration in my future writings. You can leave a review on Amazon, Goodreads or Barnes and Noble.

Your thoughts and opinions mean a lot to me. Also, be sure to check out my website and social media sites for upcoming books and giveaways.

Sincerely,

Mary Theriot

Links

Website www.maryreasontheriot.com

Goodreads for reviews -
http://www.goodreads.com/MaryReasonTheriot

Facebook - http://goo.gl/Sd0VgY
Twitter - @Mktheriot

Google+ - +MaryTheriot

YouTube - http://goo.gl/ErM1M6
Pinterest - http://www.pinterest.com/mktheriot

Blog Page - www.maryreasontheriot.me